COUNTING STARS IN DURHAM

ADAM LAWRENCE

AL PUBLISHING

— · —

DISCLAIMER

This is a work of fiction. All names, characters, businesses, places, events, and incidents in this book are either the product of the author's imagination or used in a fictitious manner. Any resemblance to actual persons, living or dead, or actual events is purely coincidental.

1

---·---

APRIL 12TH

Duke University's West Quad was quiet as Allison and I strolled hand in hand on a beautiful spring Sunday morning. I was nervous as I rolled a felt box in the pocket of my shorts. A clear blue sky soared overhead. The white magnolias were in full bloom, releasing their sweet, citrus-like scent.

Last week, during spring break, I flew home to New Jersey to buy Allison's engagement ring. We usually spent our vacations together, but I made the excuse that I needed time alone to study for my medical school entrance exams.

When I arrived home, I visited my father's longtime jeweler. The choices of diamonds overwhelmed me: the shape, the clarity, the color. I drummed my fingers on the glass display case as the saleswoman showed me options. "Do you think she would like a princess cut, round cut, or oval cut?" "Did I care more about the size or the clarity?" I looked at her blankly. The rings all looked the same to me. I settled on a basic half-carat round diamond in a plain gold setting. The engagement ring was reminiscent of Allison's unpretentious and understated personality.

Allison's ring cost twenty-five hundred dollars . She deserved a bigger diamond, but I was over my maximum budget. I had saved two thousand from my part-time work as a paramedic. I put the balance on my credit card, knowing I would need to work extra shifts upon my return to North Carolina.

I stopped in front of the soaring Duke Chapel and pretended to study its Gothic architecture. The church was the defining landmark of the University's campus. I took Allison's hand and led her up the eight slate steps from the quad to the grassy area in front of the church. I couldn't hear any other noises than the pounding of my heart. I wiped my sweaty palms on the back of my shorts.

"Why are we going up here?" Allison asked.

"I just want to see something," I replied vaguely. Sunday morning services were taking place in the Chapel. I could hear the enormous pipe organ playing inside— a musical testament to God's power.

As we climbed the steps, I stopped on the penultimate ledge, letting Allison reach the top. Then, in traditional fashion, I kneeled on the hard stone. Allison took several steps before she realized I was no longer alongside her. She looked down and saw me holding out the ring to her.

"Will you marry me, Allison?" I took a deep breath and briefly felt horrified. Did I propose marriage? I had turned twenty-three last week, and here I was getting engaged. Growing up, I thought I might want a life partner but never kids or traditional wedlock. My three-and-a-half-year relationship with Allison had changed my mind. I could not imagine graduating from Duke without having her permanently in my life.

Allison put the ring on her left hand and held it up to the sun. She watched it sparkle as the beams of light bounced through the prism of the diamond. She took my hand, pulled me up, and threw her arms around my neck.

"Of course I will marry you, Adam." She grinned and gave an uncharacteristic yelp of excitement. Allison was never one to show her feelings in public. Her career as a champion figure skater had taught her that emotion had no place in competition. She could not show happiness, anger, or pain on the ice. Even after her skating career ended, she approached her life with dispassionate determination. Today, however, on the steps of Duke Chapel, she beamed with happiness.

"I'm sorry the diamond is so small, but it was the best I could do for now. I promise I will upsize it in the future."

"Adam, it's perfect." She moved towards me and kissed me softly on the lips. "I love you so much. I'm happy we're going out into the world together."

Four students sitting on the grass erupted in applause. Allison and I both laughed in embarrassment.

"Congratulations!" one woman yelled. "You go, boy!" shouted another. I looked at the ground, shook my head, and smiled. Serendipitously, the bells of the Duke Chapel rang from the towering carillon, celebrating the end of Sunday worship.

"Let's go back to my room. I have to call my mom and my sister!" Allison was nearly skipping in happiness as we headed back to her dorm.

Holding hands, the engagement ring rubbed conspicuously against my finger. My emotions were mixed: panic and happiness, trepidation and hopefulness. The proposal had gone better than expected, but now there was a wedding to plan. I would vote for elopement, but I knew that would never fly with Allison's family.

Allison's dorm room was quiet when we returned. Her roommate Julia had gone away for the weekend. While clothes were strewn across Julia's bed, Allison's side of the room was spotless. Her shoes were tucked neatly under the bed, and the sheets were folded with crisp corners.

I closed the door and moved to kiss Allison. I slipped my hand around her waist, pulling her into me. She pushed my arms down and away.

"Not now. I have calls to make."

It was the perfect time for intimacy—a beautiful April Sunday morning. We had just gotten engaged, and her dorm room was empty.

"Come on, Allison. Let's celebrate our engagement." I kissed her neck, but she swatted me away like an irritating fly.

"Adam, I said not now!" She paused, knowing she had spoken harshly. Her voice softened, though it was clear she was not interested in sex. "I want to tell everyone about our engagement. Let me make my phone calls, and then we'll see what happens."

Disappointed, I slipped off my shoes and lay on Allison's bed. I stared at the white square ceiling tiles as I tuned out Allison's conversation with her mother.

I remembered the previous summer Allison and I spent in Europe. For eight weeks, we traveled through Italy. The summer semester was a requirement for my degree in classical studies. For Allison, it was a means to use her college scholarship to explore the world.

After the formal program was over, Allison and I spent two weeks exploring the rest of Italy. We hiked along the Cinque Terre, explored the churches of Florence, and walked the canals of Venice.

For the finale of our trip, we took a train to Nice and spent two days on the Côte d'Azur.

On our last day in Nice, we took a short stroll from our hotel to the beach. The clear Mediterranean Sea reached out towards North Africa. The temperature was eighty degrees, with a light breeze blowing off the water. Unlike the United States, there was no white sand on the beaches, only hard, rounded stones.

We laid our woven mats on the rocks, which were nicely cooling in the heat. Allison turned on her back and opened her iPad, holding the tablet between her eyes and the sun. I was uncomfortable on the rocks, so I leaned on my side and looked around. Three women in their early twenties lay down next to us. They were American, talking loudly about a party from the night before. All three girls took off their bikini tops and lay bare-chested on their mats. I tried not to look but couldn't resist peeking.

Allison caught me staring at the girls. "Like what you see?"

"I'd like it more if you took your top off."

Allison snorted in reply. "There is no chance of that. Keep looking over there if you want to see boobs."

I turned onto my stomach and pulled a towel over my head to block the sun. The warmth of the French Riviera lulled me into a deep sleep. I woke up with a dry mouth and drool running down my face.

"Was I asleep?"

"For the last forty-five minutes. You woke up everyone on the beach with your snoring." Allison wore earplugs whenever we slept in the same bed. "I'm getting hot. Let's go back to the hotel."

"One thing before we go." I rolled towards Allison and kissed her on the lips. She kissed me back. I was surprised. Typically, she allowed only a peck on the cheek in public.

"Come back here," she said. We kissed more, and I became adventurous. I ran my hand up her smooth legs to her thighs. I cupped her chest as we kissed, and to my surprise, she did not push me away. The French Riviera had loosened her inhibitions.

"Let's go back to our room," Allison said, shoving her iPad and towel in a beach bag as I rolled up our mats. She smiled at me seductively and whispered, "I want you now." We hurried to our hotel, which was two blocks away.

Turning onto a narrow street, we found the building with its green wooden door. The sun streamed into the lobby through an open atrium, though a fading linoleum floor darkened the room. The man behind the desk waved as we went up the curving staircase to the second floor.

I kissed Allison on the neck, and she giggled as she opened the door. She crossed the room and opened the shutters. We could see the sun glinting off the blue water. A soft breeze from the Mediterranean filled our room.

Allison looked incredible in her bikini. Her stomach was flat with well-developed abs. Her arms and legs were toned to perfection. She was muscular but, in every way, feminine.

We made love twice, the bed squeaking through each session. This was the most active I had ever seen Allison during sex, and I loved every second.

When we finished, we spooned facing the window, the afternoon sunlight pouring over us. We lay in bed for the rest of the evening until the sun was replaced with cool darkness. Music rose through the streets from nearby cafes and bars.

"Ready for dinner?"

Allison rolled over and smiled. "Let's go one more time." What a way to end our semester abroad.

When we flew back to North Carolina at the end of the summer, our sex life returned to bland and vanilla. I understood that sex was always more exciting on vacation, especially on the French Riviera. Perhaps our lack of intimacy was caused by the stress of school or living in dorms. Allison pushed me away more than she reciprocated my advances. Despite Allison's rejections, I loved her immensely. We connected on a deep emotional level and could talk all night. We shared the same values and the same political views. She accepted me for my many faults.

Allison hung up with her mother and smiled at me from her chair. "My mom and dad are so excited."

"Wonderful. "My voice ballooned with sarcasm.

Allison rose from her chair and sat next to me on the bed. She leaned over and kissed me. I put my arm around her and pulled her body against mine. She resisted, pushing herself back up.

"I still have to tell my sister about us." She paused, sensing my disappointment. "I promise it will only be a few minutes." Allison and her sister never talked for less than an hour. I returned to staring at the ceiling, wondering if I had made the biggest mistake of my life.

2

MAY 15TH

A month later, the North Carolina sun shone down over Wallace Wade Stadium, a concrete arena on the Duke University campus. The graduates, clad in black gowns, sat silently in the heat. Rows of students sat in semicircles on the football field, some of whom had decorated their caps with dollar bills, crosses, or the words "MOM."

Behind us, on the metal bleachers, sat our families and friends. On the stage in front of us, the president of Duke was finishing his speech. He discussed our responsibilities to our communities and families. It was uninspiring at best. As the president finished, scattered applause arose from the graduates and the audience. Most people in the crowd were too busy fanning themselves to clap.

The president introduced Ellen Rose, a well-respected television journalist, who started her speech by asking us to stand and applaud our families for their support during our education. We listened to her recount her rise from a weather girl in Cincinnati to a nightly news anchor whom America trusted to deliver unbiased reporting.

My nylon graduation gown stuck to me in the heat. I peeled it off my arms and legs. Allison and I sat with our hands intertwined. Although we had moved into our new apartment last week, today marked the end of college. Tomorrow, Allison and I would officially be in the real world, outside of Duke's gothic cradle.

Loud applause and yelling snapped me back to the present. The keynote speaker had finished, and the audience was on its feet. Finally, the president of Duke took the podium again. He thanked Ellen for her dedicated work in journalism. After a few more brief remarks, the president yelled, "Congratulations! You are all graduates of Duke University!"

With that statement, cheers broke out among the graduates. Some threw their caps in jubilation. I dropped mine on the field since it was soaked with sweat. Allison stood proudly. She was living her dream, graduating summa cum laude from Duke.

Allison threw her arms around me. "Adam, are you ready for our future?" This wasn't a question. It was a statement of our new reality.

"I'm ready to go anywhere with you." I had no idea where the next year would take us. Allison had her entire life planned. My uncertain career path presented an ongoing tension in our relationship. Although I had majored in Classical Studies, I planned to attend medical school, but I wasn't sure that would ever happen. My science grades were mediocre, and my standardized test scores were average. In contrast, Allison had already been accepted to Duke Medical School but deferred her admission for a year to continue her work with HIV patients.

With a mix of happiness and apprehension, I walked off the football field, holding hands with Allison. As we transitioned into our lives outside Duke, I was worried that, despite my love for her, I could never give her the life she wanted. She would be a doctor, no doubt at the top of her graduating medical school class, while I plodded along as a paramedic on the streets of Durham, unable to meet her expectations for a husband.

3

— · —

MAY 16TH

After the graduation ceremony, Allison and I celebrated with our own families. Allison's family had chosen an informal cafe feasting on North Carolina barbeque, hushpuppies, and sweet potato pie. As my parents were divorced, I was forced to split my time between my mother and my father. This was nothing new to me. My parents divorced when I was three, and I have no memories of them living together.

Since my mother and father couldn't tolerate sitting at the same table, I was subjected to two dinners that night. My mother had made reservations at a restaurant that served high-end Southern cuisine, while my father had chosen the most expensive steakhouse in Durham.

I arrived at my father's dinner as he and his friends were ordering dessert. Despite my parents' divorce, my father was always involved in my life. He coached my Little League teams and attended my school plays. We went out for dinner once a week, and I stayed at his apartment every other weekend. We both loved baseball and would go on a two-week road trip every summer to watch games across the country. My father was not a warm man, so those summers were the closest I ever felt to him.

By the time we finished our desserts, it was 10:00 P.M. I said goodbye and headed home. I fell asleep on the couch, waiting for Allison.

The clock read 12:30 A.M. when she walked through the door. I couldn't help but stare when she walked in. She was wearing a blue sundress with bright red and yellow Caribbean colors. The thin straps of the dress showed off her toned upper arms. The dress hugged her thin waist to her mid-thighs. She wore blue strappy sandals, which added two inches to her height. The colors played perfectly off her light blue eyes and corn-blonde hair. At that moment, Allison looked the most beautiful I had ever seen her.

"Tired?" I asked as I met her at the door. She laid her head on my shoulder, and her breath smelled slightly of wine. I kissed her on the side of the neck. "Too tired?"

"Not at all."

I took her hand and led her into the bedroom. I unzipped the back of her sundress, and it fell to the floor. I wrapped my hands around her back to unsnap her bra, but she pushed them away.

"Why don't you get into bed, and I'll join you in a minute?"

I lay anxiously under the covers, pulsing in anticipation. Before undressing any further, Allison turned off the bedroom lamp. She switched on the bathroom light and closed the door, letting only a sliver of illumination into the bedroom. I blinked, adjusting my eyes to the darkness. Allison turned her back towards me and unsnapped her bra, letting it fall to the floor. I studied the curves of her back and the shape of her hips. Before she took off her underwear, she slid under the sheets.

Throughout our relationship, I never saw Allison completely naked, save for our time in Nice. She was always covering some part of her body or had the lights turned low during sex. Allison's body image was a collateral effect of her figure skating career. Skating was only for petite girls; no chubbiness was allowed on the rink. Around the apartment, she always wore flannel pajamas or a fluffy robe. After sex, she always dressed quickly with her back to me.

Once under the covers, she turned towards me, and we kissed again. I ran one finger down her spine and heard her moan softly. I ran my hands between her legs, but as soon as I got to the top of her thighs, she squeezed them together tightly.

"Get your hands out of there!"

I tried a different tactic. I kissed her neck and moved lower on her body, kissing first along her right collarbone and then her left. I kissed her between her breasts and then around her belly button. I moved lower. I kissed the inside of her thighs, hoping I could give her a different type of pleasure.

"What are you doing, Adam?" We had only engaged in oral sex once during our four years together. It was a night when we were both smashed after one of her sorority parties. For Allison, oral sex, either giving or receiving, was a dirty activity.

"Stop, Adam! Get back up here!" She pulled my head from between her legs.

I pushed myself to the top of the bed. We went back to kissing and eventually made love in the missionary position. I tried to flip her on top several times, but she resisted, preferring to remain on the bottom. I enjoyed watching Allison orgasm, and her head arching back, but the sex left me unsatisfied.

Our sex was boring and uninspired. It took care of her needs, but not mine. I craved other positions, other places outside the bedroom. I wanted exciting, passionate sex while we were young.

When we finished, Allison quickly got out of bed and went into the bathroom, carrying her pajamas. I listened through the door as she performed her bedtime rituals: brushing her teeth, flossing, and gargling with mouthwash. Allison returned to bed, slipped under the covers, and turned away from me.

"Good night," Allison said, her voice filled with sleepiness. I slid towards Allison and wrapped my arm around her. "What are you doing?"

"Loving on you."

"Well, get off me. I want to sleep."

I sighed and rolled over. We lay back-to-back in bed. Allison snored softly. I wanted to feel her body heat against me. Instead, I stared at the wall in frustration until I fell asleep.

4

MAY 25TH

The United States Olympic Figure Skating Exhibition had come to Raleigh, North Carolina. Allison had bought tickets six months ago. She had planned to bring her sister, but Faith's senior prom was the same weekend, so I was attending as her stand-in. I didn't mind going with Allison, but I had no interest in watching figure skating. I was a football and baseball guy; I never understood the draw of the Olympics.

We arrived at the arena half an hour before the exhibition started. I hadn't seen Allison so excited in quite a while. On the forty-minute drive, she talked nonstop about her work in HIV outreach. Her job entailed tracking down patients who tested positive for HIV but were not yet taking medications. She would call them on the phone, visit their houses, and locate them at homeless shelters. Allison talked with such passion about serving this population.

I didn't mind that she talked about her work, but I didn't understand most of what she said. What Allison knew about HIV was far beyond my scope of knowledge. I tried to pay attention, but I found myself confused and uninterested. She talked about work until we reached our seats, never once asking about my job.

Allison sat transfixed through the entire performance, studying each skater's performance. Occasionally, she would tap me on the arm and ask me what I thought about a particular move, twirl, or landing. I spent most of the time people-watching and trying not to fall asleep. Despite the loud music, my eyes closed in boredom.

At one point, Allison poked me in the shoulder. "I can hear your snoring over the music." She glared at me and went back to watching the show.

When the exhibition was over, Allison and I walked back to our car. She talked about the different skaters, most of whom she had competed with during their rise to the United States Olympic Team. At sixteen, Allison had been the number three ranked figure skater in the U.S. She was not only a shoo-in to make the U.S. Olympic skating team but also to win a medal. One week before the final Olympic tryouts, she landed awkwardly in practice, shattering her right ankle. She required surgery, and by the time she was cleared to skate, the Olympics were over.

Allison had sunk into a deep depression after her injury. The twelve grueling years she had spent chasing her Olympic dream had resulted in nothing. She claimed she had accepted her injury as fate, but as I heard her speak on the way out of the arena, I could tell she still felt a lingering sadness.

On the ride home, Allison talked excessively about the skating exhibition. I had found the whole event boring, and Allison's commentary even more tiresome. Every so often, I said "uh-huh" and "right" to feign interest.

"What should we do for dinner?" I interjected.

"I'm not hungry."

"You haven't eaten since breakfast. We could stop for sushi."

"I just want to go home, Adam."

Allison turned up the music on the car radio and stared out the window. I tried to discuss the upcoming week but only got one-word answers, so I resigned myself to finishing the ride home in silence. When we reached our apartment building, I trudged up to the second floor behind Allison.

"I'm going to shower," Allison said. I found leftover Chinese food in the fridge and ate at our small round wooden table. I waited for Allison to come out of the bedroom. Finally, at 9:00 P.M., I opened the bedroom door and saw Allison already under the covers. She had given no notice that she was done for the night.

I sighed and opted for the uncomfortable couch, another night spent apart from my fiancée. As I fell asleep, I questioned my life decisions as Allison and I seemed to grow farther apart each day.

5

MAY 27TH

As I left for work two days after the figure skating exhibition, my shoulders and neck ached from sleeping on the couch. Allison and I had barely spoken since the event. Yesterday, Allison drove to High Point to meet her mom for lunch and go antiquing. I spent the day alone, watching baseball. I wished I had friends I could call on my day off, but, except for Allison, I was alone in North Carolina.

In college, Allison consumed my social life. I never joined a fraternity or other social group. Many people become lifelong friends with their college roommates. My freshman year roommate, Ashley, could not have been more different from me. I was a suburban kid from New Jersey. Ashley was from a town of a hundred people in the mountains of western North Carolina. He spoke with a thick Southern drawl, making him sound like he was talking at half-speed. Although his accent could easily be interpreted as uneducated, Ashley was anything but. He had graduated as valedictorian from the most elite private high school in North Carolina and attended Duke on a full scholarship.

After a few weeks of living with Ashley during my freshman year, I learned I would have two roommates: Ashley and his fiancée, Tina. Tina often stayed over in our dorm room with them both sleeping in the same bed. Throughout the semester, she would come and go, sometimes staying for just one night and sometimes for a couple of weeks. Living in a cramped dorm room with Ashley and Tina was certainly uncomfortable. After the first year, they moved off campus. I lost touch with Ashley, but last I heard, he had graduated with a double major in mathematics and physics. For the rest of college, I lived in a single room.

At 6:45 A.M., I arrived for my shift at the main station of Piedmont EMS. I parked across from the ambulance bays, grabbing my black steel-toed boots and gear bag out of the trunk. My unhappiness about my relationship with Allison faded when I started my shift at 7:00 A.M. When I entered paramedic mode, I felt like I was in a different world.

My colleagues at Piedmont EMS were unlike anyone I knew, especially Duke students. Most of the EMS clinicians had only a high school education. In my eyes, this lack of formal education did not degrade them. I felt like my coworkers were my people. I preferred spending time with my fellow first responders to Duke's pretentious students. There was no sense of entitlement. There was no whining. EMS had operating procedures and protocols to follow. The expectation was to follow them or find another job.

There was also cursing, pranks, and a general sense of camaraderie. Spending twelve-hour shifts with a partner in stressful situations forged an inevitable bond. I responded to housing projects and dilapidated houses infested with cockroaches. I saw assaults of all types: shootings, stabbings, baseball bats, and even a golf club to the head.

When I mentioned these experiences to my acquaintances at Duke, they looked at me incredulously. I imagined they asked themselves, "Why would he ever put himself in those situations?" Duke was a great university, but I did not fit in well. During my junior year, I trained as a paramedic at a local community college. I had much more fun in my medic classes than I ever did in my classes at Duke.

My patients respected me, and most were extremely thankful for the work I did. I considered a career as a paramedic and passing on medical school. I could have made decent money and had a fulfilling life, but I doubt Allison would have approved.

My partner George and I were working on Medic Two for the day. George was close to sixty years old and had a shape that could best be described as spherical. After spending his EMS career eating a fast-food diet, he struggled to climb in and out of the ambulance. We all thought it was time for him to retire after his knee replacement last year, but he showed up at work each day as we waited for his heart attack.

Today was my first shift working alone as a paramedic after completing my three-month probationary period. I was now responsible for all clinical decisions made during patient care. No preceptor would check to ensure I was giving the correct dose of medication or review my EKG interpretation. I was in charge of the care provided in the ambulance. I, a twenty-three-year-old, two weeks out of college. I was nervous as hell at the thought that one of my decisions could kill an innocent patient.

George was not the partner I had hoped for on my first solo shift as a medic. Even the most experienced paramedics depended on their EMT partners to back them up. A knowledgeable EMT assisted with patient care and acted as a crucial backstop against clinical errors. I was lucky if George could push the stretcher into the house.

After completing our equipment checks and fueling the ambulance, we met the crew of Medic One at Biscuitown, a chain breakfast restaurant near our base. Medic One and Medic Two both worked out of the main station, where the administrative offices for Piedmont EMS were housed. It was Monday morning, which meant all the administrators and supervisors would be working. When the "white shirts" were around, there were bunk rooms to clean, supplies to sort, and training modules to complete. There would be no lounging, naps, or goofing off. We avoided returning to the base as much as possible during the day, but our absence would also be noticed.

The smell of fried food and grease filled the restaurant. Danielle and Wayne, the crew of Medic One, were sitting across from us in a booth. I knew Wayne well. He had been my preceptor during my probationary period. Wayne had been a paramedic for over twenty years and had seen it all. Nothing fazed him: gunshot wounds, car crashes, or cardiac arrests. His favorite phrase was "fucking old people" whenever we were dispatched to a patient over the age of sixty. Wayne played as if he didn't care, but he was one of the best medics at Piedmont EMS.

I didn't know Danielle well. Though we had worked at the same station once or twice, we were never partners. Looking across the table, I noticed her dark green eyes and a slightly crooked smile. Our eyes briefly met, lingering a bit longer than expected, but I didn't get the impression she was flirting with me.

Most mornings, we met at Biscuitown for one of the unhealthiest meals imaginable. The namesake breakfast biscuits were filled with warm butter that melted perfectly into the flaky dough. The biscuits were served with creamy gravy and hash browns, covered with a generous amount of salt. We did not get our caffeine boosts from coffee. Instead, we all had large Styrofoam cups filled with iced tea, sweetened with buckets of old-fashioned cane sugar.

As we ate the last bites of our breakfast, a harsh tone blared in unison from our radios. "Medic One, respond to 852 North Main Street, for a seventy-six-year-old man with chest pain."

Wayne and Danielle sighed as they crumpled their breakfast wrappers onto their plate.

"Fucking old people," Wayne said on cue. "Are you sure you don't want this one? Sounds easy. You never know what's next."

"Enjoy," was my one-word response as I smirked and leaned back in my seat.

George sucked the last bits of his iced tea through a straw with a slurping sound. I threw my garbage in an overflowing trash can and walked into the steamy morning air. It was not yet 9:00 A.M, but the temperature had already hit ninety degrees; it was forecasted to hit one-hundred degrees by noon. I watched George amble across the parking lot, huffing and puffing, gagging on the summer air. He grunted as he climbed into the ambulance.

"Take your time getting back to base," George muttered, closing his eyes and leaning against the door frame.

We were only half a mile from the main station, so I turned down a side street to delay our return.

"George, what is that?" I poked him in the shoulder. Gray smoke billowed from an apartment complex. □□

George cracked open his eyes for a few seconds, then closed them again. "Looks like we got us a fire."

The Triangle Court apartments were rows of nondescript two-story structures. As I rounded the corner, I could see flames billowing from the roof of one of the buildings. People were milling around on the grass, pointing at the fire. No one seemed in a particular hurry to move away.

I unclipped the microphone from between the seats. "Medic Two, Dispatch," I tried to convey a sense of urgency.

"Go ahead, Medic Two."

"Medic Two reporting a structure fire at the Triangle Court apartments, 330 North Pleasant Avenue. Smoke and flames are visible. I'll get the exact building but start rolling the fire department."

"Roger, Medic Two. I'll put the fire department route."

I drove slowly past the burning apartment building. I tried to figure out which building was on fire but couldn't make out the lettering.

"George, can you see what building that is?"

George yelled to a man standing on the sidewalk. "What building is that?"

"L," he replied. "Are you going to put that out?"

George grunted and motioned with his thumb, "Ambulance, not fire truck."

The closest fire battalion was only a mile away, and I could hear the sirens as they pulled out of their station. "George, we need to check if anyone is still in those buildings."

George showed no inclination to get out of the ambulance. He leaned his head against the door with his eyes closed. "The fire department will be here in a few minutes."

I heard an explosion as I jumped out of the ambulance and ran toward the burning building. Part of the roof had collapsed onto the second floor. The noxious smell of burning plastic filled the air.

Building L had eight apartments, four on each level. I went to the first apartment on the lower level and banged my steel flashlight on the hollow front door. "EMS! Is anyone in there?" There was no response.

I went to the next apartment and tried to open the screen door. I yanked it, but the owner had nailed it shut. As I approached the third apartment, a woman in her sixties emerged in a pink housecoat.

"Do you know if anyone is living in these apartments?" She shrugged and hurried off into the crowd.

As firefighters pulled hoses towards the blaze, I knew it was time to retreat. I watched the flames engulf the second floor of the apartment building. The entire roof had collapsed, and the structure was likely to fall. I coughed a few times as black smoke irritated my lungs. Gray ash fell from the sky. There was no saving the structure or anyone inside.

Our responsibility now shifted to providing medical care to the firefighters. George had pulled the stretcher out of the ambulance and turned the air conditioner on full blast in the back of the truck. It was our responsibility to keep these firefighters safe.

By now, there were forty firefighters on the scene. A ladder truck extended high in the air, pouring hundreds of gallons of water per minute onto the fire. Torrents of water ran down the street, my boots parting the channels of water like the Red Sea. The battalion chief directed the first arriving firefighters to rotate to rehab, which signaled them to come to the ambulance, cool down, and have their vitals checked.

The first firefighter climbed into the ambulance. I helped him out of his air pack and turnout jacket, which together weighed forty pounds. The second firefighter climbed in, and I helped him do the same.

"How are you guys doing?" They both nodded okay, but I wouldn't expect anything else. We sat silently, the cool air blowing from the ceiling, the clock ticking away. They were antsy, wanting to return to their battalion. They couldn't wait to go back to their jobs. Fires were what they lived for.

The firefighters extinguished the blaze within three hours; they spent the rest of the time checking for hot spots and confirming no victims were inside. Around 6:30 P.M., we cleared the fire and headed back to the base. Half an hour later, we handed the ambulance keys to the oncoming overnight crew.

My uniform smelled like I had been at a barbecue. My hair was coated with bits of debris that had sprinkled down from the sky.

My first shift alone as a paramedic had gone as well as could be expected. I hadn't killed anyone, and my performance gave me confidence for the next day. We had supported the firefighters, and they all went home uninjured. I was proud to have played a part in keeping everyone safe.

As I drove home, the confidence that I had gained during my shift was replaced by anxiety. How would Allison treat me when I walked into our apartment? Would she be happy to see me at home, or would I spend another night on the couch? At work, I was the medic in charge of the ambulance. With Allison, I felt subordinate.

Could a marriage succeed with such a power imbalance? My anxiety turned to sadness as I pulled into a parking space in front of our apartment. I hoped my fiancée would be waiting for me, but I expected another night of loneliness.

6

—·—

JUNE 4TH

It was 8:15 P.M., and I was supposed to have finished my shift over an hour ago. I drummed my fingers on the door handle as Jennifer headed north on Main Street. She drove faster than usual, cruising through a yellow light without slowing down. We were both eager to get home, as we had to be back on shift in the morning.

At 6:45 P.M., Jennifer and I had been dispatched to a chest pain call in a rural area of Durham County. We both sighed as the alert tones went off. Neither of our relief had shown up early for the evening shift, forcing us to take the late call. The overtime pay was not worth the hours added to a busy shift. These late calls were a known hazard in EMS. We could never count on leaving our shift on time. We missed romantic dates and children's baseball games. We missed birthday patients and kids' school plays.

Brian, the oncoming paramedic, was waiting for me when we parked the ambulance in the bay. "Let's get you out of here." I frowned. Had he shown up fifteen minutes early to his shift, as was custom, we could have done this transition an hour and a half ago. We transferred the controlled substance box and initialed the paperwork to verify that the vials were present and unused.

The evening had cooled down nicely, and the breeze smelled of the incoming rainstorm. I cracked the window to let in the fresh air. It washed over my face, keeping me awake on my drive home. After listening to sirens and chatter all day, the quietness was a welcome change. Twenty minutes later, I pulled into a parking space beside Allison's beat-up Toyota Camry. I found Allison sitting on the couch, reading a book. I kissed her on the back of her neck, but she jerked away.

"We had a late call. There was nothing I could do."

Without looking up from her book, Allison said flatly, "Your dinner is in the kitchen." A bowl of pasta and a glass of iced tea sat on the counter. I looked back at Allison; she was still reading.

In the bedroom, I changed out of my uniform and took off my thick work socks, letting my feet breathe from the dankness. I sat on the bed with my eyes closed, enjoying the stillness. As the positive memories from work faded, they were replaced by the disappointment at the unenthusiastic reception I received from Allison. When I came home, I expected her to be excited to see me or at least interact with me. I sighed, hoping that when I returned to the living room, she would show some emotion that suggested she was glad to have me in her life.

Walking back to the couch, I stood behind Allison and put my hands on her shoulders. I rubbed her neck, feeling the tiny knots rolling and popping between my fingers. "How was your day?"

"Fine," she muttered, not making eye contact.

I craved Allison's feel and taste. After a long day at work, I wanted to kiss her. I wanted our bodies intertwined. Undeterred by her first rejection, I sat on the couch and leaned my head against her face, her book still in her hands. I tried to kiss her, but she pushed me away.

"Stop it!"

"What's wrong?"

"I'm reading. Go eat."

It had been like this since the skating exhibition. There had been no touching, no kissing, no sex. At night, we lay together in bed, back-to-back. We could have as easily been mistaken for roommates rather than two people engaged to be married.

I sat at the table, eating cold pasta. I was physically exhausted and didn't have the energy to heat it in the microwave. Allison was still buried in her book.

"Are you mad at me?" She didn't respond. "I'm sorry I got off late. I couldn't help it."

She finally looked up. "That's what you always say," she said.

I banged my fist on the table in anger. The plate rattled, and the glass of iced tea fell over, brown liquid running onto the floor.

"I can't control the late calls. I'm sorry if my blue-collar job isn't good enough for you."

Allison stood up and went into the bedroom, slamming the door.

"Fuck," I said quietly, angry at myself for my outburst.

I remembered a chilly November night eight months ago, when I felt closest to Allison. I had walked from my dorm to Allison's, weaving through a series of Gothic archways. When I reached the second floor, Allison's door was cracked. Quietly, I pushed it open. She stood with her back to me, a white towel wrapped around her head. She wore dark blue jeans and a black turtleneck, a style she favored in colder weather. The clothes fit her snugly, not in a provocative way, but in a manner that showcased her subtle sexuality.

I watched in the doorway as Allison unwrapped the towel from her head and pulled her blonde hair back into a ponytail. I never dreamed that I would have a girlfriend this beautiful. Tip-toeing across the room, I put my hands on Allison's waist and kissed her on the cheek. She spun around and gave me a radiant smile, then kissed me lightly on the lips.

"Ahem," I heard from behind me. I dropped my head. Julia was in the room; her bed was behind the door, so I hadn't seen her when I walked in.

"Hey, Julia," I said, not turning around. Julia was Allison's roommate and best friend at school. They had lived together during their first year at Duke and remained roommates for the rest of their college years. The problem was that Julia and I couldn't stand each other. I wasn't sure why she disliked me so much. We were both from New Jersey and grew up twenty minutes away from each other. Our high schools were sports rivals, and she was friends with several people in my graduating class.

I knew why I disliked Julia. She took every opportunity to badmouth me, making it clear that Allison deserved better. According to her, I wasn't smart enough, good-looking enough, or successful enough to be with Allison. Despite knowing that Allison and I had been dating for three and a half years, Julia tried to set up her on multiple dates.

I pressed my forehead against Allison's, still with my back to Julia. Allison and I stared into each other's eyes and smiled.

"What are you up to tonight, Julia?"

"Reading for my women's studies midterm. This book would be a good read for you, Adam. It's about..." I shut out Julia's voice. Her voice was grating, and it carried an air of superiority.

"Walk?" I whispered in Allison's ear. She nodded.

As Allison put on her coat, Julia prattled on about feminist literature. I had no interest in or understanding of what she spoke about. She preached, expounding on how men had fucked up the world. All I heard was "Wah, wah, wah."

Even though the November night was only slightly cool, Allison dressed as if she were going to the Arctic. She put on a puffer coat, a pair of gloves, a plaid scarf, and a wool hat with two long cables tied under her chin. The hat framed her face, emphasizing the softness of her cheeks and the one dimple on her left cheek.

"We'll be back soon," Allison said to her roommate.

"Behave, you two. No fooling around."

"Julia, we always behave." I took Allison's hand. "In terms of fooling around, we already did that yesterday," I paused for effect, "On your bed."

Allison pulled me out of the room laughing as I heard Julia scream, "You mother...." We sprinted down the hall and into the stairway.

"Why did you tell her that?" Allison laughed. She rarely showed this much levity.

"I was tired of listening to her spout bullshit."

I thought Allison would be angry. She hated talking about sex, even when it was just the two of us. She smiled and kissed me. "I love you, Adam."

We walked out of the dorm into the cool night air. With Allison's scarf around her neck, I could only see her blue eyes and the pink tip of her nose.

"Where do you want to go?" Allison pointed towards the library. We walked slowly in the cold, Allison leaning against me to stay warm. This felt so right: how our bodies fit together; how we smiled at each other knowingly while Julia gave her sermon.

Our feet crunched on the fallen leaves as we walked on the quad. A crescent moon shone through the crisp night air. Spotting an enormous pile of leaves next to the library, I dove in, pulling Allison with me. I wasn't sure of Allison's reaction. She was the opposite of spontaneous, planning out each step of her life with deliberate intention. To my surprise, Allison laughed.

The bed of yellow, red, and brown leaves created a cozy nest. Covering ourselves with a blanket of leaves, we lay on our backs without saying a word. We heard people walking by, but we couldn't be seen, our bodies sunk in the massive pile of leaves. Allison's scarf was still pulled up over her mouth. I took her gloved hand in mine and pulled her scarf down. I touched her cheek with the back of my hand. Lying with Allison in the leaves felt perfect.

"I love you, Adam."

I kissed her on the lips, then on the tip of her nose.

"I love you, too."

We lay in the leaves until well after midnight. I went to get up, but Allison grabbed my arm. "Let's stay a little longer." We covered ourselves in leaves, pressed our bodies against one another, and drifted off to sleep.

A car alarm from the parking lot outside my apartment jerked me out of my reminiscence. I looked at my phone. It was 10:30

P.M., and I had to get up in seven hours for my shift. I opened the bedroom door quietly. Allison was asleep on her stomach, gently snoring, her arms above her like goalposts. I thought about climbing into bed, but I was sure that would only wake her, and then she would be annoyed when my alarm went off in the morning. I opted for the couch, pulled a fleece blanket over me, and drifted off to sleep.

7

— • —

JUNE 14TH

Allison and I had felt the stress of our first month living in the real world. We both knew we needed to reconnect. She agreed to take two days off work, and we flew to the Jersey shore for a long weekend. My family had a condo at the beach about an hour north of Atlantic City.

Wednesday night, Allison and I flew from Durham to Newark, hoping it would rekindle our relationship. As we drove the hour from the airport to the beach, our lives felt like they were meant to be. We laughed, singing along to music from our teenage years. We rolled down the windows as our car flew down the highway through the summer darkness. I felt free, intoxicated by love. A car honked as I rolled over the dividing line into the next lane. I had been too busy looking at Allison's smile than paying attention to the road.

An hour after we left the airport, we pulled into the condo's underground parking garage. Taking the elevator to the fourth floor, we walked into the sparsely decorated apartment. I opened the door onto the terrace and stepped into the night air. A cool breeze blew in from the ocean, giving me goosebumps. Innumerable stars dotted the black horizon. A large freighter bobbed along in the water; in the distance, it was no bigger than my thumbnail. I could hear music playing from a restaurant on the beach, the patrons dancing shoeless on the sand.

Allison stood in front of me, trembling with a chill. I put my arms around her. She pressed the back of her head into my chest, and I held her closer. For a change, life felt right: Allison, the stars, the ocean air. We stood for minutes on the balcony, enjoying each other's touch. This was the love I remembered. This was the closeness I craved.

Surprisingly, Allison led me into the bedroom. We undressed to our underwear before slipping under the covers. We faced each other, our mouths intertwined, my hands exploring her body.

"Adam, will you be angry if I say I don't want to have sex tonight?" I frowned, and Allison noticed the frustration on my face. "Adam, I want to enjoy being near you tonight. I promise we'll have sex in the morning."

I smiled and buried my disappointment. We kissed in bed until we both started yawning. She lay with her back towards me, and I curled around her. I draped my arm over her chest, and she grasped it with both hands, pulling it against her. I felt the warmth of her breath blowing on my arm and the heat from between her legs.

This is how I dreamed of my life with Allison. This is how I wanted to fall asleep every night: wrapped around her with our bodies melded as one. For the first time in a month, I slept peacefully, fully relaxed, floating weightlessly in bed.

8

— · —

June 16th

Allison and I spent the weekend enjoying each other's company and listening to the sounds of the shore. During the day, we lay on the sand until the afternoon sun became too hot. We walked shoeless at the water's edge, our bare feet sinking into the wet sand, creating footprints only to be washed away by the next wave. We strolled along the boardwalk in the evening, people watching and enjoying ice cream. At night, we fell asleep in each other's arms.

On Saturday, it rained the entire day. We spent the morning in bed, making love twice, and listening to the thunderstorms roll by. In the afternoon, we lay together on the couch, binge-watching TV shows we had missed over the last year. For dinner, we ordered Chinese food and never left the apartment. We ate on the sofa, sharing food from the square containers while we laughed at the TV.

I knew these opportunities would not last. In a year, Allison, would be in medical school. Our lives would be consumed by pathophysiology, embryology, and the clotting cascade. We would have no time for vacations and outings. I wanted to enjoy this beach trip, knowing how our lives would soon change.

On our flight home from Newark to Durham, Allison held my hand and leaned against my shoulder. She hadn't held onto me like this since Nice. I put my chin on her head as she nestled into my chest. I, too, felt calm.

Our beach trip was the fix we needed to get our relationship back on track. Landing in Raleigh, I felt like Allison and I could plan our wedding again. We had reconnected and reminded each other why we had been together for four years. Our love had been restored, and I was confident we could head into the future together.

9

JUNE 24TH

The morning had been quiet for a Monday, usually the busiest day of the week. We only ran three calls in the first six hours of our shift. After dropping off our last patient at the Duke Emergency Department, Wayne and I drove to East Campus. We pulled into a paved area where we could see the entire quad. From there, we watched.

Although graduation was six weeks ago, the quad was filled with college students. Women lay out in bikinis while others played a co-ed game of ultimate frisbee. Their shorts and sports bras left little to the imagination.

Besides its reputation as the Harvard of the South, the weather and the girls were the main reasons I ended up at Duke. I had received a full scholarship to Brandeis University in Boston, but I despised the cold. I applied to Duke, never having visited the campus, but knowing the weather was warmer in the South. What I knew most about Duke was its championship basketball team.

When I received my acceptance letter to Duke in February, I flew to North Carolina to tour the campus. When I left Newark airport, I wore gloves, a parka, and a wool hat. A gray sky hung over the dirty snow that had accumulated over the previous week.

When I arrived in Durham, it was cool but comfortable. By the time I toured the campus the next day, the sun was shining, and students were walking around the quad in shorts and T-shirts. Classes were sitting on the grass discussing literature and politics. I couldn't help but gawk at the girls who were only a few years older but seemed so much more mature than we high school kids. After that visit, there was no doubt in my mind that I was going to Duke.

The ambulance radio crackled. "Medic Seven, respond to 4008 Oak Avenue for an injured person." I sighed, not wanting to leave our fantastic viewpoint.

"Guess we need to take off." Wayne slid on his wraparound sunglasses as I marked us responding on the laptop. The call was for a female with a head injury. The GPS showed a twelve-minute response time, and Wayne was in no hurry. He sang along with country music on the radio, his voice raspy from years of smoking.

Fifteen minutes later, we pulled in front of a dilapidated house. A large group of people were arguing on the front porch. I saw one man throw a haymaker punch at another. His enormous belly protruded from under a tank top that was two sizes too small. Most of the other men had already taken off their shirts.

"Did anyone mention a fight?" Wayne asked. I looked back at the laptop. There was no mention of a disturbance in the dispatch report. "We need to get the fuck out of here until the police arrive." He shifted the ambulance into drive.

"Hold on!" I yelled at Wayne, grabbing his arm. I pointed to a woman lying on the grass. She wasn't moving. I tried to see if she was breathing, but from our distance, I couldn't tell.

"Medic Seven," I said into the microphone.

"Go ahead, Medic Seven."

"Were the police dispatched here? We have a fight in progress."

"Let me check." The dispatcher paused. "No police dispatched."

"Then send them code three."

"About ten minutes on your police unit."

I looked back at the woman lying on the ground. She still wasn't moving. Twelve minutes was a long time. The men and women were still shoving each other on the front porch. Two large pit bulls barked aggressively on the porch behind a metal gate.

"How do you want to play this?" I asked Wayne. One tenet of EMS is scene safety: never enter a situation where you, as the medical provider, could be put at risk of harm. Seeing the injured woman in front of me made me reconsider this supposed black-and-white principle.

"We gotta drive around the corner until the police get here."

"We can't leave that woman. She could be dying."

"I don't want to be dying either."

"I'm not leaving her!" I put on a pair of purple gloves and opened the door. I may have been young and inexperienced, but I would not abandon this woman. She could be bleeding to death or have life-threatening head trauma. Our job was to treat the ill and injured, and that was what I planned to do.

Wayne grabbed my arm. "Don't be a fuckin' hero. We'll both end up hurt." I pulled my arm away and climbed out of the ambulance. "Fine. Just fuckin' great." As much as Wayne did not want to get hurt, he would not leave his partner alone. "Let's grab her, get her in the fuckin' ambulance, and get out of here."

There was a lull in the fighting, and now everyone was screaming at each other. Wayne and I hurried across the front lawn towards the patient, trying to cover the thirty feet as quickly as possible. I kneeled next to the woman who was lying on her back. Bright red blood oozed from a cut on her head. Her eyes were open, though she wasn't moving.

I shook her gently on the shoulder. "Are you awake?" She turned her head to look at me. She blinked but said nothing. "What's your name?" I asked, trying to gauge her level of alertness. I scanned the rest of her body and did not see any other injuries.

Wayne crouched behind me, watching my back while trying to remain out of sight. It didn't work.

"Get the fuck off my lawn!" a man screamed at us. "Get the fuck away, you motherfuckers!"

I looked up at the porch. The eyes of the crowd were now focused on Wayne and me. "We gotta go," he whispered. Wayne put his hands in front of his chest in a gesture of peace to the crowd. "We're not the cops. This lady's hurt, and we want to take her to the hospital. That's all."

"I'm the one who hurt her, motherfucker!" a large man yelled back.

The two pit bulls scratched the metal gate. Now, I was scared. If the police didn't arrive within the next two minutes, we could be seriously hurt.

I looked back at Wayne. "Grab her shoulder!" he yelled.

I grabbed under her right armpit, and Wayne grabbed her left. The woman was dazed but managed to support some of her weight.

"Fuck!" yelled Wayne as a forty-ounce glass beer bottle whizzed by his head and shattered on the sidewalk. Voices on the steps taunted us. An empty beer can hit me in the back.

"Let's go! Let's go! Let's go!"

We had about ten yards to cover before we reached the ambulance. The crowd stayed on the porch for the time being. Maybe they just wanted to put on a show and scare us. Dragging the woman, Wayne and I scampered over the grass. We opened the back door of the ambulance, which shielded us from the crowd.

We lifted the injured woman into the back of the ambulance and wedged her between the stretcher and the bench seat. There was no time to secure her. I dove into the back, falling on top of the woman. In the distance, I heard sirens coming, but they were still minutes away.

Suddenly, I heard "ping, ping" off the side of the ambulance. Then there was a thud and a splat.

"Fuck me! They're shooting at us!" Wayne yelled.

I couldn't see anything from the floor of the ambulance. Wayne didn't take the time to close the back doors before sprinting to the driver's side. He stepped hard on the gas; after a lurch, the tires gripped the asphalt and accelerated forward, leaving black marks on the road.

We ripped around a corner, the ambulance's back doors wildly swinging back and forth. As we took a tight turn, my head hit the stretcher. I felt dazed and nearly vomited from the erratic movement of the ambulance. I clung to the stretcher, hoping this horrible ride would be over soon.

After seven minutes that felt like seventy, the ambulance turned hard to the left and skidded to a stop. "Medic Seven, Dispatch, we relocated to the Gas and Go on Eighth Avenue!" Wayne yelled into the radio. "Send us police and another ambulance code three."

A few seconds later, Wayne appeared at the back door. We were safe. Bystanders gathered around, wondering why an ambulance had flown into the parking lot with lights and sirens, its back doors wide open.

I sat on the floor next to the captain's chair, trying to slow my breathing. Sirens blared as police cars from different agencies pulled into the gas station at high rates of speed.

"You okay, man?" Wayne asked. I nodded, but my hands were shaking uncontrollably. I felt my heart pounding against my ribs like I was being punched with each beat. My breathing was rapid causing my fingers and toes to curl.

Wayne helped the injured woman onto the stretcher. She was crying, her face buried in her hands. "What's your name, sweetie?" I had never seen Wayne speak so compassionately to a patient. He reached out and held her hand. "You're safe now. We're all good."

She looked up at Wayne. "Alana." The girl continued to sob. I taped a piece of gauze on her head to stop the bleeding.

Dispatch had sent everyone to assist: the North Carolina State Police, Durham County Sheriff's Department, and Durham Police Department. At least ten police cruisers were parked haphazardly in the gas station. I saw another ambulance pull in, followed by our EMS supervisor.

Jennifer and George stood at the back of the ambulance. Wayne spoke in a soft voice. "This is Alana. We haven't checked her out completely, but it looks like the cut on her head is the only injury. Can you take her to the emergency department?"

"No problem."

"Alana, this is Jennifer," Wayne said, still holding the girl's hand. "She and her partner will take you to the hospital to be checked out. They'll take good care of you."

Wayne helped Alana down the rear step of the ambulance. The young woman squeezed Wayne's hand. "Thank you for helping me," she said. From the tone her voice, there were not many people in the world looking out for her.

Standing next to the ambulance, I counted ten small divots on the side of the truck. The white paint had been blown off, revealing the gray metal underneath. The pings I heard were BBs ricocheting off the ambulance. Three pink paintball splotches also dotted the side of the ambulance.

Wayne lit up a cigarette and took two long puffs. I had heard of paramedics being attacked by patients or ambulances surrounded by crowds, but I had never heard of ambulances being shot at. Real bullets would have pierced the side of the ambulance, killing us both. I had made a mistake by putting Wayne and me in danger. I regretted my decision to jump impulsively out of the ambulance rather than heed Wayne's warnings.

Wayne put his arm around my shoulder. "You are one stupid motherfucker." He slapped me on the back and walked over to our EMS supervisor. I think "stupid motherfucker" might be the highest praise Wayne gave out to his partners.

After a few minutes, I stopped shaking, but now I felt the urge to cry. I buried my head in my hands and fought back tears. I had never come this close to death before. That I could have been killed was not hyperbole.

My thoughts turned to Allison. Would she care that her fiancé had nearly died? I had hoped that when I told Allison about my day she would hold me in her arms, but I feared she would tell me it was part of my job and that I should deal with it or find something else to do.

Allison and I had returned home from our beach vacation with renewed energy for our relationship, but as our week progressed, we fell into the same cycle of anger and resentment. With each passing day, I felt our future slipping away and doubted we would ever see our wedding night.

10

— · —

JULY 16TH

Allison and I had no plans for this beautiful summer Sunday. We ate breakfast and headed to Eno River State Park. We had hiked the Eno River many times during our four years at Duke. It was a perfect place to spend time alone. The park was outside the city, away from traffic and noise, but only twenty minutes from campus.

A peaceful forest with winding trails interlaced with slow-moving streams. We hiked for several hours, stopping to sip from our water bottles. Each time we stopped, I tried to kiss Allison, but I was met with her cheek rather than her lips. At one point, we sat on rocks and dipped our toes in the river. Tiny fish circled between our feet.

Occasionally, a hiker crunched by on the path above us, but large green ferns hid us from view. We sat enjoying the peace of the gurgling river and the clean smell of the forest. Allison showed little emotion, staring stoically into the stream. I reached out and took her hand. She didn't pull away, but she didn't look at me. Why was she so frigid?

"Everything okay?"

"Uh-huh."

"Are you sure?"

"Yes," Allison responded curtly. We were alone in a beautiful, relaxed setting. I touched Allison's cheek, trying to turn her face towards me, but she resisted. I twisted my body around so I could kiss her on the lips.

"What are you doing?"

"Trying to kiss you."

"Well, keep your tongue out of it."

I shrank back, insulted. This was the perfect secluded spot for an intimate moment. Maybe not sex, though I wouldn't have been opposed. At least we could kiss. No one could see us, yet Allison was hesitant. I pressed my lips to hers and ran my hands up her back.

"Would you get off of me?" she growled.

"Did I do something wrong?" I didn't understand why she was resisting.

"I'm not in the mood. Especially not here." To me, this was the perfect place to start something romantic. Without saying another word, Allison stood up and headed back to the parking lot. I watched as she strode away. I waited two minutes, though it felt like twenty, hoping she would look back.

Was this to be our life together? No hugging or kissing, even when we were alone. I had a high sex drive, but nothing abnormal for a twenty-three-year-old man. What did she expect?

Nonetheless, I didn't want to give up on Allison. We had spent nearly every minute of the last four years with one another. We studied together, traveled together, and ate most of our meals together. Our lives had become entwined, and I couldn't fathom unraveling our relationship. I loved Allison and wanted to spend my life with her. I hoped if I loved her enough, our intimacy could develop.

Finally, I followed her down the path. I could make out Allison's pink tank top as she walked the trail in front of me. She showed no signs of slowing down. After ten minutes, I caught up to her in the parking lot.

"Ready?" she asked.

We sat silently in the car on the ride home. Thirty minutes later, we arrived at our apartment. I took out two glasses from the kitchen cabinet and filled them with water from the refrigerator dispenser. I handed one to Allison. She took a long sip.

"I'm going to take a shower," she said. I smelled myself and was grossed out. I needed one too.

Allison went into the bedroom and shut the door. I heard the water running from the shower. This was the perfect time for us to be naked together. We rarely showered together during our relationship, but now we were in our own apartment.

When I opened the bathroom door, I saw Allison peeling off her sports bra. I took off my T-shirt and moved in quickly, holding the sides of her waist. She jumped backward and covered her chest with her arms.

"What are you doing?" she asked angrily.

I stepped in closer, put my hands on the small of her back, and pulled her towards me. "I thought we could shower together."

"Get out!"

"Come on, Allison. Now is the perfect time to have some fun."

"You just don't get it! Get out of here! Jesus Christ, Adam!"

I backed out of the bathroom dejectedly. "Do you want to have sex when you get out?" She slammed the door in response.

I never understood why Allison was so resistant to sex and nudity. She was beautiful, and by any standard, had a perfect body. I imagined it was related to her Southern Methodist upbringing.

We had now shared an apartment for two months. We were already arguing over sex, which did not bode well for the next fifty years. Before proposing marriage, I should have waited to see how our lives functioned beyond the Gothic walls of Duke. I figured our relationship would improve as we settled into a routine, started our new jobs, and shared the same space. Instead, we drifted apart every day, our relationship spiraling downward from love to indifference.

11

— • —

SEPTEMBER 12TH

I sat against the wall of our apartment, tears running down my face. I sensed what Allison was about to tell me: "Adam, this isn't working, us living together."

I thought back to when Allison and I met during our first week of college at an orientation program called Project Build. The program offered new students the opportunity to get to know one another while serving the citizens of Durham. During the day, we built houses. At night, we talked, played games, and watched movies.

I met Allison on the second night of Project Build. She was unlike anyone I had met before. With blonde hair and blue eyes, she spoke with a slight Southern accent. It was sweet and cultured, exotic sounding to a boy from New Jersey. Allison and I quickly became friends during that week of orientation. We spent most of our nights talking on the enormous wooden bench outside the dorm.

Allison and I did not see each other during the first few weeks of our freshman year. She joined the crew team, which started practice at 5:30 A.M. She spent the rest of the day in classes and often studying late into the evening. Although we lived in the same dorm, we rarely crossed paths unless we passed each other on the staircase. I would try to talk to her, but she was always rushing to class, the gym, or the library. A month later, we reconnected during a social night in our dorm. After a game of Pictionary, Allison and I ended up lying in the middle of the quad, counting the starts of each constellation. That night was our first kiss. From then on, we were inseparable. We ate our meals together, spent time together on weekends, and traveled together during school breaks.

I should have realized that a marriage between Allison and me could never work. We were two vastly different people. Her parents never accepted me. I was not who they expected their daughter to marry. They wanted Allison to marry a man who could match the drive and grit she had developed through competitive skating—a man with a clear path to success in life.

When I visited Allison's family, I spent most of my time alone in her room. Her father never invited me to watch a football game or play golf, and her family ignored me during meal conversations in the small kitchen nook.

I hated those trips to Allison's house in Greensboro. I felt uncomfortable the entire time, exiling myself to the guest bedroom. Her family showed no interest in having me there. I spoke as little as possible, making excuses to run errands to get out of the house. Allison told me I was paranoid, but she overlooked her parents' extreme indifference towards me.

Why did I ask Allison to marry me if we were so different? I never dated casually. In my romantic life, I had always been all in. Marrying Allison was the next logical step to maintaining our relationship after college. I was too young to understand the folly of my thinking. Everything works swimmingly when you aren't in the real world. The university provides meals and housing. There are no arguments over electric bills or work schedules.

Now, four months after graduation, I sat in our apartment crying as she handed her engagement ring back to me. I refused to take it, so she laid it on the floor next to me. I cried. I begged her to stay.

"How can you do this to me?" I yelled at her. I cursed at her, and then I cried again. I sat against the door to prevent her from leaving.

I tried to process Allison's reasons for breaking up. She said she needed more life experience before getting married. Why couldn't she have figured this out in May before she said yes? Why did she need anyone other than me?

After sadness, I cycled through anger. I had never cheated on her. I had a degree from Duke and a solid job as a paramedic. I screamed, "How can you walk out on me? We were meant to be together." I yelled more, and she yelled back. I stood up and balled my fists. I slammed them against the wall over and over, like a hammer trying to ram a nail into a small hole. I threw the sofa pillows across the living room, knocking the TV off its stand.

I cried, and then she cried. We cursed at each other again and yelled more until we both realized nothing was being accomplished. She walked out the door, taking a suitcase with all her clothes. "I'll text you when I'm coming to get the rest of my stuff," were the last words she said.

That was the end of our engagement—a diamond ring on the floor next to me instead of on Allison's finger. I was alone in North Carolina, with no friends, no family, and an empty apartment.

Next to the front door was a small wooden table where we placed our keys upon entering the apartment. On the table was a framed photo of Allison and me from our summer in Italy. I slammed it on the floor, shattering the glass. I threw the frame like a Frisbee across the room. The corner hit the wall, leaving a quarter-inch hole. I felt some of the broken glass dig into my foot.

More than the physical pain, I felt the emptiness of being alone. I had no friends here save my acquaintances at Piedmont EMS, and I never saw them outside of work. Despite our lack of intimacy, I knew Allison loved me. If I were sick, she would take care of me. If I was traveling alone, Allison would chew her nails until my plane landed safely. Even if our sex life wasn't great, I was still sharing a life with someone else.

I lay on the floor, imagining that I was looking into Allison's eyes, stroking her soft cheeks. I rolled on my back and sobbed for the rest of the evening until sleep overtook my emotionally drained mind.

12

OCTOBER 2ND

In the three weeks since Allison left, my time was either spent at work suppressing my feelings or at home wallowing in sadness. Allison had picked up the rest of her possessions but left me the couch since it was too heavy for her to move. She took the TV stand, so my television was stacked on cardboard boxes that I had found in the recycling pile at my apartment complex. I still had the small dining room table, two chairs, and my bed. She took some pity on me since we had purchased those items jointly. All other traces of her were gone: her clothes, her lotions, her facial scrub. All the art on the walls was hers, so now the inside of my apartment was white plaster walls with nail holes, a persistent reminder of my emptiness since Allison had left.

I picked up so much overtime that I worked eleven days straight. At least I was getting out of the apartment. I had stopped exercising. I only left the house for work. Living in that apartment, I couldn't forget Allison. Our relationship may not have been perfect, but I had someone to share my life with.

Now, I was alone in Durham. I could break my lease and move back to New Jersey. But what would I do there? I could try to get a job as a paramedic, but with the government bureaucracy, getting a New Jersey license could take months. Living with my mother at twenty-three was not an appealing choice.

I ate leftover pizza for dinner while watching Monday night football. Everything felt empty: the apartment, my mind, my soul. My uniform shirt and pants lay crumpled on the floor. Depression surrounded me. I didn't have the energy to brush my teeth and get ready for bed. I set my phone alarm for 5:30 A.M. and pulled a fleece blanket over my head to block out the light. After an hour of restlessness, I fell asleep, my mind craving a calm night's rest.

13

OCTOBER 28TH

The blaring klaxon jerked me awake from my post-lunch nap.

"Motor vehicle crash, Durham Freeway at mile marker three in the median. Multiple injuries."

I walked into the ambulance bay and around to the passenger side. George shoehorned himself into the driver's seat. As we responded, we heard the scene size-up: four cars were involved, with one overturned.

We entered the highway half a mile from the crash. Already, traffic had come to a stop. We moved all the way to the left, and the ambulance vibrated as we rode along the rumble strip. I could see the emergency vehicles arriving from the other direction: fire trucks, police cars, and a highway traffic truck, its yellow arrow directing drivers to move over.

When we arrived at the crash, it was like no scene I had encountered. Cars and people were scattered throughout the wide, grassy median. Everyone was yelling and pointing at someone who needed help. There was a distinct smell of gasoline. Firefighters rushed around the scene, triaging patients to show who was the most severely injured.

We had participated in tabletop exercises in EMT school. We were given a hypothetical mass casualty incident. Red tags indicated the most severely injured patients, while green tags marked the least injured. Even worse was the black tag, a patient who was dead or had no chance of surviving their injuries. I hoped I never had to decide who was destined to die.

Now, at an actual mass casualty incident, I stood frozen, holding the trauma pack in one hand and an oxygen tank in the other. Traffic crawled slowly, and each driver seemed to stare at me. Noise disappeared; there was a high-pitched ring that filled my ears.

One firefighter directed me towards two patients lying on the grass. "Get these two out of here first! They're both red tags!"

I kneeled in the mud next to the woman, wet dirt soaking into my knees. Both women were talking, a good initial sign. I found out they were mother and daughter. The mother was the driver of the overturned car and had been ejected through the side window. Her breathing was labored, but she was moving her arms and legs. The daughter was bleeding from a large gash in her head. She had crawled out of the car through the shattered windshield.

George appeared next to me, carrying two yellow plastic spine boards. He dropped them next to the patients. If he kneeled, he might not get back up.

"Give me the collars!" I shouted. "Let's get them on the boards and go!"

George flagged down two firefighters to assist us with moving the patients. I applied a collar to the mother's neck while one of the firefighters applied another to the daughter's. Gently, we slid the mother onto the backboard, and the firefighters carried her to the ambulance.

I spoke reassuringly to the daughter while I waited for the firefighters to return. I felt the pulse in her wrist—a little fast, but not unusual considering the circumstances.

"What's your name?" I asked the young woman. I could see the white of her skull through the deep cut in her forehead.

"Brianna."

"What grade are you in, Brianna?"

Through the tears and the mud on her face, she uttered, "tenth."

"What's hurting you?"

"Just my head."

George and the two firefighters returned. We rolled Brianna onto a yellow longboard and tightened the straps around her chest. We added a block around her head to keep her neck stable, then placed her in the ambulance. Brianna's mother had already been secured to the bench seat.

I sat in the chair at the head of the stretcher. From my seat, I watched the mother and daughter reach their arms out and squeeze each other's hands. Brianna's mother tried to turn her head to see her daughter.

"No, no. You need to keep your neck still."

The back doors of the ambulance were still open. I was mesmerized by the hundreds of flashing emergency lights. I heard my pulse in my ears, and my temples pounded.

The slamming of the ambulance's back doors woke me from my haze. "Are you ready to go?" George yelled from the front of the ambulance.

"Two trauma patients to Duke, code three! Give them a heads-up!"

We were about seven minutes away from Duke Hospital. There was no time to start IVs or perform other invasive treatments, especially with two patients crammed in the back of the ambulance speeding down a bumpy interstate. The best treatment for Kayla and Brianna was rapid transport to the hospital.

I felt the ambulance bounce as we pulled out of the median and onto the highway. I attached a pulse oximeter to Brianna's finger and the blood pressure cuff to her arm. Her oxygen saturation was 100%, and her blood pressure was 132/68, a solid number. I inspected the cut on her head. The deep laceration was oozing, but there was no arterial bleeding. I pressed gauze onto her head and covered it with a large piece of tape.

I touched Brianna's mother on the shoulder and reassured her that her daughter was okay. Her breathing seemed more labored, but she was still awake. I slipped an oxygen mask over her face. I could see the fear in her eyes as she stared at the bright fluorescent lights embedded in the ambulance ceiling.

I remembered my EMT training when I was strapped to a hardboard and driven around in the ambulance. Lying on the rigid plastic spine board was excruciatingly painful. I felt suffocated by the cervical collar, which was taped to the board so that I couldn't move my neck. As we moved, the ambulance tilted from side to side, making me feel as if I were about to fall onto the floor. With each bounce, the plastic board dug farther into my skin. Although I hated the experience, I could tell my patients I understood what it felt like to be on that board.

The ambulance bounced into the driveway of the Duke Hospital Emergency Department and backed into a parking space in front of the ambulance doors. "We're at the hospital," I said to

Brianna and her mother. "There'll be a few bumps as we get you out."

George appeared at the back door of the ambulance. He turned to another crew who had just dropped off a patient.

"Can you get the woman on the bench seat onto your stretcher and get her inside?"

We rolled Brianna into the trauma bay. The trauma team, a cadre of doctors, nurses, and technicians, had already gathered inside. The trauma bay was an equalizer. All patients received the same protocolized trauma care. All clothes were cut off, and every crevice was explored for injuries. Rich or poor, Black or White, every patient was treated the same in the trauma bay.

I had warned Brianna that it would be loud in the trauma bay and that there would be lots of people asking her rapid-fire questions. The most embarrassing moment for the sixteen-year-old girl would be when they would strip her completely naked to check for injuries. I could not imagine a more mortifying experience for a teenager.

"Everyone, no talking!" The order came from Dr. Lisa Jones, the Chief of Trauma Surgery at Duke. Dr. Jones was a petite woman with short gray hair and a huge personality. She was the first female trauma surgeon at Duke and was well known in the Durham community for her advocacy against violence. Despite her thin frame, she was one of the most intimidating women I had ever met. I was nervous simply thinking about giving her a report.

I stood in the designated EMS spot at the end of the bed. "Sixteen-year-old female, no past medical history, restrained passenger of a car that rolled over at high speed on the Durham Freeway. She crawled out of the car on her own. Her only visible injury is a head laceration down to the skull. Her heart rate was 110, and her blood pressure was 132/68, GCS fifteen."

"Thank you," Dr. Jones said dismissively, making it clear my talking time was over.

"The next patient is more critical," I told Dr. Jones, but she was no longer paying attention.

George wheeled Brianna's mother into the adjacent trauma bay. Dr. Jones stood at the foot of the bed where she could see both patients.

"Same thing," Dr. Jones ordered. "Get the patient moved over and let's hear the story."

I gave my report to the trauma team and was quickly dismissed by Dr. Jones. When I returned to the ambulance, George was wiping blood off the stretcher. I sat on the back step with the rear doors open as I typed the patient care report on a laptop. Wayne and Jennifer joined us by our ambulance. Wayne held a lit cigarette, which he puffed directly in front of the no smoking sign nailed to the hospital wall.

Jennifer was Wayne's partner on Medic Three. She was twenty-nine, blonde, with a bubbly personality. She was also single and enjoyed sharing the details of her dating life, whether we were interested or not. Jennifer loved to gossip and had a finger on the pulse of everyone's social situation at Piedmont EMS. Most importantly, though, she was an excellent EMT, and starting on the next rotation, she would be my usual partner.

Jennifer sat down next to me on the back step of the ambulance. "Who's going to the Halloween party?" She was met with silence. "You know I'll be there," Jennifer said after no one answered.

"What are you dressing up as this year?" Wayne asked. Last year, Jennifer dressed in an elf costume. Her top was extremely tight, and, as I heard secondhand, her large breasts fell out several times during the party. Although she was the talk of Piedmont EMS afterward, Jennifer didn't seem to mind. She enjoyed the attention and often sized down her uniform shirt to make it fit a little more snugly.

"I'm thinking some sort of alien. Are you going, Adam?"

"Honestly, I don't know anything about it."

"Are you off Saturday night?"

"Yes."

"I'll text you the address. Don't worry about dressing up." She paused, leaning in close to my ear. "I know that you've been sad since your fiancée left. Get out and meet someone new."

I looked at her, my mouth slightly agape. Jennifer had gone back to typing on her laptop. How could she know about Allison? I may have mentioned my breakup a few times at work, but never when Jennifer was around.

Wayne and Jennifer climbed into their truck and turned on the ambulance. Diesel fumes filled the air. Wayne waved through the open passenger window. "See you at the next one."

"I'm going to check on them," I told George.

Considering that it was my first mass casualty incident, and I was simultaneously treating two critical trauma patients, I had done a decent job. Even though I had provided little clinical care during the call, I had stayed calm. I had empathized with both mother and daughter, which was not easy since Allison left. I found it difficult to be kind to patients when I was hurting so much inside.

As I walked into the emergency department, I saw a nurse standing in the trauma bay, restocking equipment for the next patient. He looked up at me.

"How did they do?"

"The mother had a collapsed lung, and the trauma docs put in a chest tube. The girl had no serious injuries. She needs her head sewn up."

In paramedic school, we were taught that caring for people during their worst times was an honor. Today, I felt that sense of honor for the first time in my career. It was unlikely that Kayla and Brianna would remember me in the future, but I was certain to remember them.

I wanted to ask the nurse some follow-up questions, but the tones on my radio interrupted me.

"Medic Five, respond to 326 Main Street for a sick person." I turned around and headed back to the ambulance. I was a paramedic and proud of it. Allison was out of my life, and I could finally take pride in my work.

14

OCTOBER 31ST

Jennifer had texted me nonstop over the last two days, asking if I was going to the Halloween party. After telling her repeatedly that I wasn't going, I relented the morning of the party. I would force myself to leave my apartment rather than wallow in the anguish of my breakup with Allison.. Tonight marked my emergence from my cocoon of despair.

Allison and I were apart for the first Halloween in four years. Neither of us cared about the holiday, but her sorority hosted an annual Halloween party. We had a great time at those parties, dancing, drinking, and forgetting about the pressures of school. It was one of the few times Allison would let loose and drop her stoic exterior. ☐

At 6:00 P.M., I drove Northeast out of Durham towards an address twenty miles from my apartment. Once outside the city limits, the roads gradually narrowed and darkened. There were no streetlights, only the orange reflectors marching down the double stripe in the middle of the road. To my right and left, open fields stretched into the darkness. I could make out the faint outlines of barns and shadows of farm animals roaming the fields.

After forty-five minutes, I turned onto a gravel road marked only by a trio of mailboxes at the corner. My GPS spoke to me. "Your destination is five hundred feet on your left." I drove around a tight curve and saw a brightly lit house set back from the road. I slammed on my brakes, skidded, and barely missed striking the brick column at the entrance.

Cars were parked haphazardly in the driveway and on the front lawn of the house. I found an empty space on the grass with an easy escape route.

I turned off the ignition but remained seated in my car, questioning whether I wanted to go inside the house. I hated parties. I struggled to engage in small talk, felt awkward with people I didn't know, and even more uncomfortable with those I did. I found most people uninteresting, which didn't help my social interactions.

Since Allison left, I had even less desire to socialize with others. She was the person I would hang out with at parties. We enjoyed talking to each other rather than socializing with other party guests. Now, I was alone at this party. I decided to have a drink, say hello to Jennifer, and then leave.

A brick walk led to a beautiful old plantation house built in the 1800s. The house had large white columns and a wide sweeping porch. On this tepid October night, all the windows were open, and red curtains flapped in the windows. The house glowed orange, isolated from the surrounding darkness. The nearest house was a mile down the road. The country air felt clean, without the contamination of urban pollution.

Standing on the porch, I counted the stars, which shined brightly in the rural darkness. I imagined what it would be like to live in isolation with no neighbors in sight. Where I grew up, houses were stacked one next to another on small plots of land. I could look into my neighbors' bedrooms and watch them cooking in the kitchen.

Jack-o'-lanterns flanked the steps leading up to the house, their toothy grins flickering orange. As I climbed onto the porch, I thought again about leaving before anyone saw me. Growing up, I always disliked Halloween. Trick-or-treating in the cold Northeast October weather never appealed to me. I hated ghosts, skeletons, and everything related to the holiday.

"Adam!" A large figure rushed at me. "I didn't think you'd come." Jennifer gave me a big hug and kissed me on the cheek. Her breath reeked of beer, and her hair smelled of cigarettes.

Jennifer had dressed as a "nurse." The top three buttons of her white "uniform" were open, revealing a black lacy bra. She wore black fishnet stockings and four-inch heels. The bottom of her costume barely covered her ample backside. It was difficult to avoid staring at her enormous chest, but she was too drunk to care.

"I'm going to grab a drink," I said, hoping to escape Jennifer. Although I had forced myself to come to the party, I didn't want to talk to anyone. I would have my drink and leave.

The front door to the house was open, and I went inside. Immediately, I was engulfed by blaring dance music. About thirty people gathered in the living room, with the couch and chairs pushed to the sides of the room. A flat-screen television on the wall was covered with cheap Halloween decorations. A table with food and drinks was set in the back of the room.

The loud music overstimulated me. I listened to sports radio of news in my car. Large crowds in small spaces also made me anxious. I wasn't claustrophobic, but I disliked being crammed against other people. I always sat on the aisle at sporting events, on an airplane, or at the movies, needing to have one side unencumbered.

I saw Wayne standing next to one of the front windows, a cigarette hanging from his mouth. He blew a puff of smoke out the window and waved me over.

"Adam, glad you made it," he said warmly. "Soft drinks are on the table and alcohol is in the ice chest."

I found a bottle of hard cider, twisted off the top, and took a swig. This was my first adult party outside of college. At Duke, all the parties were the same: twenty-year-olds and lots of alcohol. Inventively, some girl would vomit on the dance floor or pass out in the bathroom.

I wandered back to Wayne, who had just lit up another cigarette. We said nothing as we stood next to each other. He stared out the window while my eyes roamed the room. Occasionally, I would nod or raise my bottle in acknowledgment of someone. I felt awkward as I swished a small sip of cider around my mouth.

Tired of the smoke and the smell of spilled beer, I went out to the porch. I found an empty swing and sat down on it. At the other end of the porch, Jennifer was laughing loudly while rubbing her breasts against a man I didn't recognize.

The rocking of the swing and the fresh air relaxed me. I closed my eyes and took another swig from my bottle. It was half full. Once I finished it, I would head home.

I felt a thump next to me, and the swing bounced slightly. I opened my eyes, surprised to see Danielle beside me. She took a sip from a beer bottle and stared at the sky. The stars were abundant. Occasionally, a meteor flew by. Where I grew up, light was ever-present. Nights when I could see stars were exceedingly rare. Here, the stars dotted the sky like glow-in-the-dark stickers on a child's ceiling.

"What's your deal?" Danielle asked, still looking into the night sky. She folded her left leg into her lap while her right leg dangled from the swing. Danielle wasn't dressed for Halloween but wore a tight black T-shirt and snug-fitting blue jeans.

"I'm not sure what you mean."

"You're way too smart to be working here, so what's the deal?" She gazed up at the sky, shooting stars filling the night.

"I'm working here for a year or two until I get into medical school."

I studied Danielle more closely in the glow of the house lights. She was petite and looked to be in her mid-twenties, with a face that showed little sign of age. Her strawberry blonde hair was pulled back into a ponytail with a black scrunchie. Freckles dotted her cheeks. She wore black sandals dotted with glass beads. Her toenails were manicured and painted a dark shade of red.

In a move I hadn't expected, Danielle leaned her head against my shoulder and pressed her body tightly against mine. Was she hitting on me? I had no idea what my next move should be. It had been four years since I had dated someone new. I draped my right arm around Danielle's shoulder. I ran my hand through her ponytail. She seemed unfazed by my touch, still staring at the stars.

As she pressed her body against me, my breath quickened. Having the woman take the lead was new for me. Allison never initiated physical contact, except for the occasional peck on the cheek.

"Have you ever noticed me?" Danielle asked. I wasn't sure what the correct response was. Was I supposed to play it cool and say, "Not really," or should I admit I had thought about her?

"Of course, I've noticed you."

Danielle looked up at me with her green eyes and smiled. "You don't have to lie, but I've noticed you. I've noticed you since the first day you started here. I've noticed you because you're smarter than everyone else here." She tapped my forehead with her pointer finger. "I find smart, very attractive."

Danielle reached her hand behind my head and pulled me towards her. We kissed for a few seconds, and she put her head on my lap. It had been months since I had physical contact with a woman. I had forgotten how arousing a simple kiss could be.

I looked around to see if anyone had seen us kiss. Jennifer was still on the other end of the porch, too distracted to notice us. Wayne was no longer smoking in the window. I closed my eyes and felt good for the first time in a long time.

Danielle set her beer bottle on the ground. She sat up and took my hand. "Come with me." Danielle motioned to a minivan parked in the driveway. She put her arm around my waist and leaned her head against me as we walked. My head was swimming. I had only drunk one hard cider, but I felt intoxicated.

"Get in," she said, motioning to the front passenger door. She walked around to the driver's side. Looking at me across the hood, Danielle sensed my hesitation. "Get in," she said again with a crooked smile.

Hesitantly, I climbed into the front seat, unsure of what to expect. Danielle put the key in the ignition and turned on the battery. Soft country music played on the radio. We sat quietly for a minute, letting the sexual excitement build

"Adam, I've found you attractive from the moment I met you. You probably don't remember that we worked together during your first orientation shift. Since I saw you again at breakfast, I haven't been able to stop thinking about you." She leaned across the car to kiss me. Our mouths locked, and we made out like teenagers.

I heard voices walking by the car. Instinctively, I pulled back.

"Don't worry. They can't see us." Danielle's minivan had tinted windows, and it was impossible to see inside in the darkness. She pulled my T-shirt out of my jeans and stroked my chest. I ran my hand across her belly. Her skin was wrinkly and pooched out slightly above her jeans, unlike Allison's chiseled abs. She moaned and kissed me harder. My hands explored her chest. I slipped my hand under her bra and caressed her breasts. They were small and firm. I played with one of her nipples. She moaned in delight and pushed her tongue deeper into my mouth.

Danielle skillfully unbuttoned my jeans. With one hand, she pulled down the zipper. "Let's get in the backseat."

With her petite frame, Danielle slipped effortlessly between the driver's and passenger's seat. She kissed my neck lightly and then nibbled on my ear. I was ticklish and squirmed. Danielle laughed mischievously.

I slipped my jeans and boxers down to my ankles. I slouched down in the backseat as Danielle straddled me, wearing only a red thong. I ran my hands up and down her back, her hips grinding against me.

"What about, you know..." I didn't want to ruin the mood by saying condom or birth control.

She smiled at me reassuringly. "Don't worry. I'm taken care of."

I felt her reach down and take me in her hand. With one motion, she slipped aside her thong and put me inside her. Her ponytail had come loose from her scrunchie, and her hair brushed against my face as she bounced up and down. Danielle had a look of sheer pleasure as she moved slowly, then quickly, then slowly again. She circled her hips, hitting her G-spot with each rotation.

I heard voices outside the car again. Someone knocked on the window.

"Who's in there?" a slurred voice asked. I sat up, panicked. But Danielle put her finger over my lips and gently pushed me back down. She sat on top of me, motionless, unbothered by who was outside. A face appeared at the window, creating an eerie shadow through the fogged glass. A hand wiped at the window. Danielle and I smiled at each other in silence.

"Who's in there?" the drunken voice asked again. A fist banged on the window. Danielle showed no sense of panic or concern.

"Let's go, you moron," said a female voice. Her voice was just as slurred as the man's.

Once the voices went away, we went back to making love. Danielle's moans became louder and louder. She threw her head back with one final grunt and fell into my chest.

After a few minutes of heavy breathing, Danielle lay on my chest. "That's better than I ever imagined, and I imagined it a lot." She gave me a quick peck on the lips and pulled up her pants.

Danielle slid open the back door of the minivan and stepped out into the night. I followed her out, stumbling, tangled in my jeans.

Danielle laughed, then squeezed my hand. "Talk to you soon, babe." She kissed me on the cheek and walked back towards the house.

What should I do now? I felt the gravel crunch between my feet as I shifted my weight in indecision. I walked back to my car and sat silently in the driver's seat. The clock said 12:23 A.M. I realized I had to be at work at 7:00 A.M. but felt no urgency to go home. After fifteen minutes of watching the stars, I started my car and made a U-turn in the driveway.

I was energized from the sex with Danielle, quite proud that an incredibly beautiful woman, who saw me as both intelligent and attractive, made love to me in the back of a van. From the first kiss, there was an intense physical connection that I had never experienced before, not even with Allison.

I drove home, lost in thought, tasting Danielle on my lips. I hoped there would be a next time when I could feel the warmth of her body against me, and I hoped it would come soon.

15

— . —

NOVEMBER 1ST

My alarm clock buzzed at 5:30 A.M. to wake me for my shift. My head pounded from a lack of sleep. The events of the prior evening were blurry. Had I had sex in the backseat of a minivan like a horny teenager? I stepped into the shower, hoping the water would wash away the fog. Bits of memories came into focus. Sitting on the porch. The back of Danielle's van. The feel of Danielle's lips and the softness of her skin.

Luckily, I was assigned to the slowest EMS base for the day. I would need a nap during my shift, and Medic Eight was just the place to take it. It took approximately twenty minutes to reach the Girard Street station. I pulled into the station at 6:50 A.M. Karen, the outgoing paramedic, was packing her equipment when I walked in.

"It was a nice night. We ran three calls, none after midnight. There shouldn't be anything missing from the truck." She handed me the radio and the box of controlled substances. "See you at seven."

I opened the garage door halfway to let in the cool morning air. At 6:59 A.M., Jennifer roared up the street in her black Mustang convertible. She hopped out of her car, her uniform shirt unbuttoned, a tight white T-shirt underneath. She looked a little groggy, but she wore her usual cheerful smile. How could she look so perky after the party last night?

"I hear you had quite a night," Jennifer commented. Before I answered, she said, "We'll talk about it in a minute."

I had no idea if she knew what had happened between Danielle and me. I climbed into the back of the ambulance and went through the equipment checklist. After a few minutes. Jennifer appeared at the back door of the ambulance. "Tell me about last night. I heard you had a lot of fun with Danielle."

"I'm not sure what you mean." I feigned confusion and avoided eye contact.

"Come on, Adam. I saw you and Danielle together on the swing."

"We were just having a drink," I said, not meeting her eyes.

Jennifer watched as I stowed the medication bag and opened the trauma pack. I checked the bag twice to avoid looking at her.

"There was a rumor that some action took place in Danielle's van during the Halloween party." Jennifer was trying to provoke a response.

I stowed the trauma bag and took out the airway roll to check my laryngoscope and blades. "I'm not sure what you're talking about. I left after one drink."

I wondered if Jennifer had bought my story. I figured the best way to get Jennifer off the topic of Danielle was to ask her questions. "How did your night end up?"

"Boring. I just went home after the party."

"Really? I saw you hanging out with a couple of guys."

"Well, things didn't work out."

I was about to ask for more details when our buzzer alarmed in the bay. My head felt like it was ringing just as loudly. "Medic Eight, respond to 2453 Girard Street for an injured person."

"You're driving, Jennifer." I climbed into the passenger seat and yawned. I hadn't bought coffee on my way to work, figuring I would make some at the station before our first call.

The call was down the street, and we were on scene in two minutes. As she climbed out of the truck, Jennifer flipped her sunglasses onto the dashboard. "By the way, Danielle texted me this morning and asked me for your number."

I smiled as I stepped out of the ambulance. I guess Danielle enjoyed last night as much as I did.

16

NOVEMBER 2ND

J ennifer and I were together at Girard Sstation the next day. We
only had one call all morning and spent the rest of the time in
the station. Jennifer watched a movie on her iPad while I napped
in the crew room.

At 12:30 P.M., my phone vibrated next to my head, waking me
from sleep. I didn't recognize the phone number, but the text read,
"Do you have time to talk?"

I stared at the message. Was it Danielle? I hoped for a follow-up
message to tell me more about the sender, but the phone sat silent.

"You should answer that," Jennifer said from the other room.

How did she hear the text message come through? My phone
didn't even beep.

"I don't know who it is!" I shouted back.

"You know who it is. She wants to talk with you about the other
night."

Did Jennifer know what happened with Danielle? If she knew,
did everyone in the department know? Jennifer was always ready
to spread a good piece of gossip.

I tapped out a text on my phone. "Who is this?" I waited for a
response, but nothing came, so I closed my eyes and drifted off to

sleep. I had just started snoring when the alarm buzzed in our crew room.

"Medic Eight. Respond to 324 Williamson Street, the United Methodist Church, for syncope." We ran this call every Sunday. An elderly woman would pass out after standing for an hour in the church.

We responded to the call with lights and sirens, though there was little traffic on Sunday afternoon. Jennifer parked in front of the church. We piled our equipment on the stretcher and rolled it up the ramp into the building.

As we walked into the church, I felt the vents on the floor blowing warm air into the room. I sweated as I pushed the stretcher down the long aisle towards the altar. The parishioners at the United Methodist Church did not sit quietly and pray. This church was raucous with preachers yelling, choirs singing, and parishioners dancing.

At the front of the church, we found an elderly lady, propped against a pew, dressed in her Sunday best. She wore a purple dress, a string of pearls, and a white rose pinned to her chest. A group of worshippers crowded around her, fanning her.

As expected, our patient had been standing for a while and then passed out. She was now awake and talking. Jennifer checked her vital signs while I attached the patient to the cardiac monitor, which showed a normal rhythm. Jennifer pricked her finger to test her blood sugar, which was also in the normal range. We told her we needed to take her to the hospital to be checked out. She protested, but all the parishioners told her to go, so reluctantly, she climbed onto our stretcher.

As we wheeled the woman towards the door, I heard the preacher ask for a moment of silence to pray for Sister Davis. After a ramp and several bumps, we loaded the stretcher into the ambulance.

"Ready?" Jennifer asked from the driver's seat.

"Nice and slow." I set up the cardiac monitor across from me and timed the blood pressure cuff to cycle every five minutes during our ride to the hospital.

My favorite conversation starter with older patients was whether they had been born in Durham. As I found out, Ms. Janette Davis was seventy-two and had lived in Durham all her life. She had been healthy until five years ago when she was diagnosed with diabetes and had a heart attack. Now her medical problems were under control, and she was an active part of her church. Ms. Davis had only left Durham once when she traveled to Washington, D.C. to march with Martin Luther King. She had spent fifty years working in food service at Duke. She began as a line cook on the women's campus and rose to become a supervisor by the end of her career.

I never mentioned to my patients that I had attended Duke. The Duke empire was built on tobacco farming, which inevitably involved slaves. Protests against Duke were common regarding wages and working conditions. Some still considered Duke to be a plantation with a wall surrounding the East Campus to keep them out.

Ms. Davis and I chatted during the transport. She told me about her children, grandchildren, and first great-grandchild. Despite her thin frame, she showed no signs of frailty. The ambulance bounced into the hospital parking lot and backed into a space outside the emergency department.

We wheeled the stretcher through the glass doors of the ambulance entrance to a podium where the charge nurse sat. As we waited for a bed assignment, my phone rang, and the same number that had appeared earlier on my caller ID came up again. From the other end of the stretcher, Jennifer mouthed, "Answer it." I sent the call to voicemail.

After we transferred Ms. Davis to the hospital stretcher, we returned to the ambulance.

"Would you please call her back?" Jennifer insisted. I dialed the number, but instead of hitting send, I pressed end. I was too nervous to call Danielle back. I didn't know what to say, and I didn't want Jennifer listening in on our conversation.

"She didn't answer," I lied.

On the way back to Girard Street, we stopped at the main station to restock supplies. "Call her," Jennifer said as she slid out of the ambulance.

I relented and redialed the phone number from my caller ID.

"Hello?" I immediately recognized Danielle's voice at the other end.

"Hey, girl," I said, trying to sound cool. "This is Adam. You called?"

She immediately lowered her voice to a whisper. "I can't talk right now, but I want to see you again soon. Text me your address." The phone abruptly disconnected.

I texted Danielle my address, but then my stomach dropped. What had I gotten myself into? What would happen when she came over? Would we still have the same intense attraction?

Jennifer opened the door and dropped several boxes of gloves between the seats. I didn't make eye contact with her; instead, I looked out the side window, trying to hide my smile.

"You did call," she said as she put the ambulance in drive. "Danielle will certainly bring some spice into your life."

If our next time together was anything like our first, this could be the start of an amazing relationship.

17

_—·—_

NOVEMBER 5TH

Three days later, there was a knock at my door. I took a deep breath, trying to contain my excitement. Unexpectedly, Danielle texted me at 11:00 A.M. to let me know she would come by early in the afternoon. I knew nothing about her other than she looked hot in a pair of jeans, and we had incredible sex in the back of the minivan. I felt so much more excited about seeing Danielle again than I ever did going home to Allison.

I wasn't sure what to expect when she arrived. Would we have sex again? Talk? Go out to lunch?

There was a knock at the door. I opened it anxiously, and Danielle threw her arms around me. She didn't say a word, and our bodies instinctively pressed against each other. Danielle was petite at five feet tall, and, although I was only five feet six, she stood on her tiptoes to kiss me. Our tongues met, swirling around.

After a few minutes, Danielle cupped my face. "Which way to the bedroom?"

We quickly undressed, and within a few minutes, we were making love. She was on top, as she would be nearly every time we were together. She ground her hips into me, moaning, her head tilted back, her lips pursed together.

We orgasmed several times, and she rolled off me onto her back. She stared at the ceiling with the sheets down around her waist, bare-chested. I ran my hands over the velvety skin on her stomach and around her breasts.

Danielle turned and patted me on the chest. "Do you have something to eat? You wore me out."

"I'm sure I can find something," I said, pulling on my shorts. I went to grab my T-shirt off the floor, but Danielle had already put it on. It was a navy Yankees T-shirt that hung down to her mid-thighs. Underneath, she wore nothing. She looked much sexier in my shirt than if she had been completely naked. What I found most attractive was her complete confidence in her body. Her freedom contrasted with how Allison always hid in the dark.

I peered into my empty refrigerator. "How about peanut butter and jelly?" I was embarrassed that I had nothing more to offer. When Allison and I were together, she made every meal. I couldn't cook anything other than pasta or make a sandwich. I ate for sustenance, not for pleasure.

"Perfect. I didn't eat today."

I took the bread, peanut butter, and jelly from the cabinet over the sink. I found a jar of pickle spears in the back of the fridge. Danielle kissed me, taking the jar out of my hand. She crunched one of the spears, the sound echoing through my empty apartment.

As I spread the peanut butter and jelly on the bread, Danielle said, "As I told you at the Halloween party, I've been watching you for quite a while. So far, you have lived up to all my expectations, but I don't know anything about you. Tell me all about Adam."

"What do you want to know?"

"I wanna know about you. I wanna know how you got so smart and how you ended up in Durham."

"Where should I start?"

"Start from the beginning."

"You really want me to start at the beginning?" I asked, taking a bite out of my sandwich. Danielle nodded. My life story wasn't particularly interesting. I thought about creating some exciting lies, but I stuck to the truth.

"I was born in a small town in New Jersey, outside New York City. I lived there for the next eighteen years until I left for college. It was quintessential suburbia. I had an easy childhood. A story that would bore you."

She put her sandwich on the plate and wiped her face with a napkin. "You're not boring me at all. I like boring. I could use boring in my life. Tell me more."

"My parents got divorced when I was young. I have no memories of them living together. Whatever memories I do have are snippets of them arguing. I lived with my mom and saw my dad on weekends. I planned to become a lawyer like my father, but he talked me out of it, complaining about his clients and the overabundance of attorneys. In my junior year, I switched from pre-law to pre-med. Because I was late in taking my medical school prerequisite classes, I had to take a year off before applying to medical school, and here I am."

"That is a very boring story." Danielle chuckled. "I know there's more. Tell me what Adam was like in high school."

"I didn't have many friends. I did homework during the week and spent the weekends volunteering for the ambulance squad. I picked the weekends, so I didn't have to be at home while the other kids were out partying. I never drank or smoked pot. As I told you, a boring life."

Danielle took another bite of her sandwich. "Tell me about your first kiss."

"Her name was Michelle. I was twelve or thirteen years old. We were dating, or whatever you call it at that age. We would go to the movie theater and hold hands. One day, we were hanging around after school. There was a nook where a payphone used to be. I got a burst of confidence, took her hand, and pulled her into that nook. I slipped her a little tongue, but all I remember is the irritating feeling of my mouth touching her braces."

"Until you told me that story, I had forgotten how awkward middle school was. Tell me about some of your girlfriends because I know you've had practice."

"I didn't have a real girlfriend until my junior year in high school when I dated a senior. We had a fun time and explored sex together. She took me to her senior prom when I was a junior. We lost contact after she went to college. During my senior year, I dated a few different girls. My crowning high school achievement was hooking up with two girls after the senior prom."

Danielle walked over to the sink and filled a glass with water. She leaned against the counter and smiled at me. I felt my cheeks flush, still not believing that this incredibly beautiful woman had come over in the middle of the day to have sex with me.

"You are so hot," she said seductively, her green eyes glinting.

Danielle opened my junk drawer.

"What are you looking for?"

"I want to learn more about you." She found a folded photo of Allison and me standing on a cliff in the Cinque Terre. It was the photo from the frame that I smashed when Allison walked out on me. I kept the picture in my junk drawer, folded in half sloppily. I had hundreds of other pictures of Allison and me in a shoebox on the top shelf of my closet. I had no idea what to do with them.

Danielle unfolded the photo. "Who is this? Am I competing with someone?"

"That's my ex-fiancée, Allison."

"How long have you two been apart?"

"It's been about two months."

"Do you miss her?" In some ways, I missed the life that Allison and I had planned together. On the other hand, sounding too positive about Allison might drive Danielle away. I took the middle ground.

"Sometimes."

"Tell me about Allison."

"Where do I start?" When I thought about Allison, I felt angry and betrayed. "I met her during my first week at Duke. She was beautiful, like no girl I had met before." I told Danielle about our relationship, our engagement, and our breakup.

Danielle sat back down at the table. "Why did you two break up? It sounds like you had the perfect relationship." She leaned forward, her interest piqued by my story.

"I should have known that our relationship would never have worked out. Allison is one of the most brilliant people I know. She attended Duke on a full scholarship. She read books for which I barely understood the Cliff Notes." I paused and took the last bite of my sandwich. "Did I mention she also got a full scholarship to med school?"

Danielle looked across the table at me. "She sounds like an incredible woman. What happened?"

"After we moved in here in May, the fighting started. You know our job as medics: twelve-hour shifts, arriving early, and often getting off late. Weekends, overnights, and holidays. Allison's workday was nine to five, Monday through Friday. We rarely had time off together. Even though she said that she understood my job, I don't think she accepted my work as a paramedic. EMS was too blue-collar for her. Allison grew more distant, and our physical relationship waned. It's amazing how different life is in the real world than in college. In October, she gave me back the engagement ring and walked out."

I put my hands on Danielle's shoulders and kissed her on the neck. She pressed her head back against my chest. I ran my fingernails up and down her back. I felt her shudder, and she led me back into the bedroom. This was so much different from my frigid experiences with Allison. Danielle wanted the physical intimacy I so desperately craved.

After another round of intense sex, Danielle and I lay in bed next to each other for a few minutes. I ran my hand through her hair. "What's your story?"

"My story?" Danielle frowned and scratched her ear. "Adam, you do not want to know my story."

"Why is that?"

"I have to get going," she answered evasively.

I ran my finger over a small scar on the lower right part of her abdomen and then touched the matching scar on the left. "Can you at least tell me what these are from? Appendix?"

Danielle kissed me on the lips and got out of bed. She wiggled on her jeans, then pulled her shirt over her head. I was still lying on the bed when Danielle gave me one last kiss. "Talk to you soon," she said as she walked out the door.

After Danielle left, I lay motionless. I had never felt such a physical and emotional connection with a woman, not even with Allison. I could feel the warmth of the sheets, still heated by Danielle's body. I could smell Danielle's scent on my pillow. I wrapped the sheets around me, feeling Danielle's body tied up in mine.

What I thought would be casual sex had turned into something more that afternoon. Even after this brief time, I couldn't imagine not seeing her again. She wanted me for me. I didn't need to be something other than who I was. Danielle did not make me feel like an animal for desiring physical intimacy. I counted the minutes until I could see Danielle again, craving the physical intimacy that brought us together.

18

— . —

NOVEMBER 30TH

I had just left the main station after a busy Monday shift. We had run nine calls in twelve hours. We had no chance to eat breakfast; I shoved lunch down my throat between calls. By the time we returned to the station, it was 8:00 P.M. I quickly packed my gear and headed out to my car.

As I drove back to my apartment, my phone rang. A local exchange appeared on the caller ID, but I didn't recognize the number, so I sent the call directly to voicemail. In a minute, my phone chimed to signal the caller had left a message. My LeBaron had no Bluetooth, so I put the phone on speaker to hear the message.

"Hey, Adam." I immediately recognized Allison's voice, which sounded more subdued than usual. "I got a new phone number. I was hoping we could talk for a minute when you had a chance." There was a few second pause. "Call me when you can." Another pause. She cleared her throat. "Just give me a call back when you can. I need to talk to you."

I threw my phone against the floor, enraged at hearing her voice. Allison and I hadn't talked since she walked out on me. What did she want now? She had the nerve to call me two months after she destroyed our engagement. What the hell?

I fought the urge to call Allison back immediately, but my curiosity won out.

"Hello?" she answered.

"It's Adam. You called?"

"Hey, Adam. I was hoping we could get together to talk." I let the silence hang between us. "Adam, are you there?"

"Uh-huh."

"This is really hard for me, but I think I might've made a mistake."

"Really?" My voice was coated with sarcasm.

"I was hoping we could talk in person. I've been thinking about you. I remembered how much fun we had traveling and spending time together."

I wanted to tell Allison to go fuck herself, but I tempered my response. "Uh-huh."

"I think we should talk in person and figure out how to get our relationship back on track."

This was a surprising turn of events. I felt ambivalent about meeting Allison. On the one hand, I hated her for calling off our engagement. On the other hand, I thought Allison and I could still have a future together. She would be an excellent mother, a wonderful life partner, and a loyal spouse.

"I'm willing to talk about it."

"Awesome, Adam. I'm so glad I'm going to see you. I'm working until five tomorrow. How about Reindeer Brew in Chapel Hill? Around six?"

"I'm working tomorrow and Wednesday. How is Thursday at seven?"

"See you then." I had almost hung up the phone when I heard Allison whisper, "I miss you, Adam."

I doubted her sincerity. I think she missed having a fiancé more than she missed me. She had thrown away the four years of our relationship. I slammed my fists against the steering wheel in anger.

In the short time I knew Danielle, I had learned what physical attraction really meant. It was not simply wanting to have sex with the other person, but the spark and the excitement of a touch. It was craving the other person as soon as they left. A single kiss that triggered uncontrollable passion.

Until Allison and I figured out whether we would restart our engagement, I would spend time with Danielle, enjoying the passion that brought us together.

19

DECEMBER 1ST

Danielle and I orgasmed together, both releasing at the same time. She had come to my apartment five times over the past two weeks. Today, Danielle's afternoon classes were canceled because of a water pipe break, so she came over at noon instead of 3:00 P.M. She always left by 5:00 P.M., sometimes even sooner. I would ask her to stay for dinner, but the answer was always no. Today, it felt nice to have time unpressured together.

"Do you want to grab something to eat?"

She turned over on her side and cradled her head against my neck. "I'm happy right here."

"How come you never want to go out anywhere?"

"Do we not have fun here?"

I frowned, unsure why she was resisting. Whenever I tried to ask about the details of Danielle's life, she skillfully deflected them.

"Do you remember when I told you my story? Now it's time to tell me yours."

"Adam, you have a fantasy about who I am, what I am, and what we could be. I don't want to ruin that for you, and I don't want to ruin that for us. Let things go where they may."

I pushed harder. "I want to know about you, Danielle."

Danielle rolled onto her back, sighed, and shook her head. "Adam, let's enjoy what we have." Why did she not want to share her life story with me? "If you want to know my story, I'll tell you, but I'm not sure it's what you want to hear. I'll understand if you don't want to see me again." What could she tell me that was so bad? "How old do you think I am?"

"Twenty-six." I actually thought she was twenty-eight.

"Adam, I turned thirty-three last month." She propped herself onto her elbow and looked into my eyes. "I have two kids, a sixteen-year-old and a four-year-old." Then she dropped the grenade. "And I'm married."

My eyes widened, and I looked away. Did she say what I thought? Married? Kids? What I thought could be a long-term relationship had just turned into an affair, complete with a husband and children. When I first met Danielle, the connection was instant: the way she looked at me on the porch swing, the passion we had when we made love, the way the world disappeared when we lay in bed next to each other. Now, I was lying in bed with a married woman, questioning my decisions over the last month.

Danielle put her hand on my face and turned my head towards her. "None of this is your fault. You didn't know about any of this. This reaction is why I didn't want to tell you."

I looked at her left hand. There was no wedding ring. There was no line. There was no sign that a ring had ever been on her finger.

Danielle sighed. "I guess I might as well tell you the whole story. I grew up as an only child in Oxford, North Carolina. My family wasn't well-off or even middle-class; we barely made it paycheck to paycheck. My mom worked part-time at a grocery store, and my old man worked for the Post Office. My parents were good church people who played cards every Wednesday night. School wasn't my thing. I wasn't brilliant, but I wasn't dumb either.

"I spent most of my junior year smoking pot and cutting classes. I dated a guy named John, who was a year older than I. By dating, I mean we were hanging out in his basement, drinking cheap beer, and having sex. I don't think either one of us ever went to class. In October of my senior year, I found out I was pregnant. You can only imagine my parents' reaction when their only daughter was knocked up and failing out of school. What would the neighbors say? And the Church? That's when they threw me out, and I moved into John's basement."

Stories like this didn't happen where I grew up, or at least they were kept hidden. As far as I knew, none of the girls in my high school had gotten pregnant. If they were, they were likely "out sick" getting an abortion.

"I had a difficult pregnancy and had to drop out of school. Haley, my sixteen-year-old, was born in June. John and I spent the next two miserable years together. Eventually, we saved enough to rent a trailer down the road from his parents. I took whatever jobs I could find: cleaning houses or babysitting. John worked random construction jobs. Whatever money we had, John drank away or spent on lottery tickets. After work, he'd get hammered with his buddies and stumble home in the middle of the night. He usually passed out on the couch until I got him up for work in the morning.

"When Haley was three, my parents died in a car accident. I hadn't talked to them for two years. It turns out the joke was on them since I inherited everything. Their deaths saved me."

I was struck by Danielle's openness and honesty. She had grown up in a world that I could not comprehend: trailers, teen moms, and dead parents. I grew up without worrying about money or food. I never had to take care of anyone but myself.

I kissed Danielle softly on the lips. "Keep going. I want to hear more."

"Are you sure?"

"Absolutely."

"It turned out my dad had a fair amount of retirement savings and a nice pension from the federal government. The house was paid off, and there was an old Buick that my mom used only for running errands in town. I moved out of the trailer and into my parents' house. I'm not sure John knew we left since he was passed out on the couch. After that day, we never talked again. He's never tried to contact Haley or me.

"Once we moved into my parents' house, Haley and I finally had a nice place with a backyard. She could attend a good school, and we had money to pay the bills. With my dad's pension money, I only had to work part-time, and I could spend the rest of my time with Haley. We weren't exactly living it up, but we weren't wondering where our next meal would come from. I went back to school and got my GED. After that, I attended community college to get my EMT certification and then my paramedic license."

There were still ten years missing from her story. "What about your husband?"

Danielle sighed, exhaling deeply. "Oh, Jeff. We met at an EMS conference about six years ago. He was divorced, had a daughter and an ex-wife who lived in Florida. I was ready to get back into the dating scene, and I was looking for a dad for Haley. We dated for about a year before moving in together. Five years ago, we went down to the courthouse and got married. Neither of us had any family to invite to a wedding. A year later, Kyle was born. Jeff has been a great provider and stepfather for Haley, although not such a great husband; that is for another time."

"I can't imagine how you handled all the shit you went through, Danielle. You are amazingly strong." I could never have survived that life.

"By the end of next year, I'll have finished nursing school. Not bad for a high school dropout and a knocked-up teen mother."

We lay quietly on the bed. I was processing what Danielle had told me during the last few minutes. She had so much more experience in the real world than I did. I admired how much adversity she had overcome in her life.

She reached down, took my hand, and kissed the back of it. "Adam, I want you to know that I don't regret this, and I'd like to continue seeing you. I'll understand if you want to stop seeing me after what I told you."

She put her head on my chest and snuggled into me. I stroked her hair while I sorted my jumbled thoughts. I was twenty-three, single, with my whole life in front of me. Could we ever have a future together? She was married with two kids. I was closer in age to her daughter than to her. At the same time I was in elementary school, Danielle was raising a three-year-old. What had I gotten myself involved in? What if I destroyed her marriage or her family with this affair?

"A penny for your thoughts."

"Danielle, you are amazing. I don't want to stop seeing you. I'd like to see more of you.

She kissed me on the end of my nose. "Good, because I want to see more of you too."

Danielle fell asleep on my chest. Her breathing was quiet and steady, and she let out a purring snore. I stroked her head. "Danielle, I will take care of you forever."

20

—·—

DECEMBER 2ND

At 7:00 P.M., I wandered into Reindeer Brew. The coffee shop had a ski lodge feel with its rustic wood walls. Heavily varnished tables were crafted from irregular pieces of lumber. The namesake stuffed reindeer head hung over the long coffee bar.

Allison was sitting on a wooden bench near the door. She stood up when I walked in. Our interaction felt uncomfortable and awkward. She looked at the ground while I looked out the window. We made a point of not making physical contact. I bought us both hot chocolate, and we sat at a booth in the front of the restaurant.

Allison was dressed in a red turtleneck sweater with a delicate gold necklace I gave her for Valentine's Day last year. I was surprised she would still wear something from our relationship. We stared out the window in silence, sipping our hot chocolates. Finally, I started the conversation.

"Why did you want to see me?"

She paused before she answered. "Adam, this is hard for me to say. You know that I have difficulty admitting my mistakes. To me, a mistake is the same as failure."

Perfection had been drilled into Allison as a figure skater. The difference between a great score and a perfect score could be one barely perceptible movement. Perfection permeated every aspect of Allison's life. Anything less than an A+ was considered a failure. A score of 98% on a test was unacceptable.

"Adam, I want to get back together."

I had played out this scenario for when she asked to come back. In one timeline, I told her to fuck off, that she had missed her chance to be with me. In another scene, I welcomed her with open arms and told her I wanted us to be together forever. I would give her the engagement ring back, and we would pretend the last four months had never happened. In yet another timeline, I made her apologize, grovel, and beg me to come back.

"Do you really think that we could get back together after all the hurt we caused each other?"

Allison took a sip of her hot chocolate. "I'm not sure how to tell you this, but I think it's the only way to explain why I want to get back together. While we've been apart, Julia set me up with a couple of guys, giving me the chance to see what dating was like. It was terrible. I realized how comfortable I was with you. I don't want to throw that away."

I didn't see Allison's explanation as a ringing endorsement of our relationship. It sounded more like she was settling for me because she didn't want to deal with the hassle of dating.

I could feel the anger in my hands as I squeezed the mug of hot chocolate. "You dump me and immediately start dating other guys? Did you sleep with them?" Allison blushed and stared down into her coffee. She nodded.

Although I had slept with a few women before college, I was Allison's first and only partner. When we started dating, her life plan did not include premarital sex. But after a party one night filled with alcohol, we found ourselves in an empty dorm lounge. We started kissing, and it progressed to uninspired sex. It was forgettable for me, but I suspect not for her. We never discussed that night again, but it lingered in the background of our relationship.

My voice became low and measured. I inhaled through my nose to suppress my rage.

"We don't have sex for the first three years of our relationship, but then we break up, and you sleep with every guy you meet. Now you want forgiveness?"

I wanted her to feel pain for what she had done to me. I saw Allison's eyes well up with tears. "It was a mistake, okay? It was a miserable experience that I don't want to repeat with another man. It fucking hurt, Adam!"

I looked away, feeling a little guilty. My relationship with Danielle only caused more confusion. With Danielle, I had passion and intimacy, but a completely unknown future. With Allison, I might have a certain future but little physical intimacy.

Allison looked at me across the table and pulled my hands towards hers. "Adam, I want to spend the rest of my life with you. I would love the ring back. I want to plan our wedding again."

My feelings were mixed. Happiness: Allison professing her love for me. Anger: Why did she have to sleep with somebody else to find that love? Relief: I could be back on track to be married. Egotism: Allison came back to me. Doubt: whether our relationship could really work.

As much as I wanted Danielle to be a passing affair while I figured out my life, I couldn't simply set our relationship aside and bring Allison back in. Danielle meant too much to me.

Allison leaned across the table and kissed me. I couldn't remember the last time she kissed me in public. "Think about it. I'm not going anywhere."

I looked silently out of the window. Despite the thirty-degree weather, three college girls dressed in short skirts and fishnet stockings passed by the window, their voices clamoring as they walked, their stiletto heels making a staccato sound on the sidewalk. A couple walked by, dressed in matching Carolina blue beanies. They stopped to kiss on the lips. I wondered whether Allison and I would ever return to that point in our relationship, unencumbered by the misery of these last few months.

"I'm willing to try, Allison," I said with little confidence.

"That's all I wanted to hear," she said, leaning over the table and giving me another kiss.

Allison and I put on our coats and tossed our paper cups into the garbage.

"I'm working the rest of the week, but maybe we can have dinner this weekend?"

"I'm working through Saturday, so maybe we can meet on Sunday?" Allison asked.

"We'll talk and find a place to eat. I'm glad we're back together."

We weren't back together, but I didn't want to tell Allison that. We had the opportunity to rebuild the life we had planned together, and I could have the long-term certainty I craved, but could I live without the passion I had found with Danielle? That passion could never be duplicated in my relationship with Allison.

I never promised exclusivity to either woman, and neither Allison nor Danielle had been exclusive with me. I decided to stay the course with both relationships and see how life unfolded.

21

— • —

DECEMBER 19TH

As I worked out on the elliptical machine in my apartment's gym, my thoughts alternated between Danielle and Allison. I loved them both, each in a different way. I loved Allison for her stability, her drive, and her loyalty. I loved Danielle for her passion, her openness, and the mind-blowing sex.

I hadn't heard from Danielle since we last met at my apartment. She hadn't texted. My calls were sent directly to voicemail. Once, she answered the phone and whispered, "I can't talk," and hung up immediately. I was anxious that she had decided to end our relationship. I couldn't imagine not seeing her.

Two people with this much sexual compatibility must have a future together. How could our physical relationship be so intense otherwise? I imagined doing with Danielle what people do in a normal relationship: eating dinner, grocery shopping, and watching TV. I imagined what our life together would look like when I was in medical school. Danielle would snuggle up on the couch as I studied my anatomy textbook. It would be such a contrast to the frigidity I had with Allison.

As I planned my imaginary life with Danielle, my phone buzzed on the table. Allison was calling to confirm our date for the next day. We had met for dinner several times over the last two weeks. The conversation flowed easily, but our physical relationship had not advanced past kissing. Although she repeatedly said she wanted to be with me, I sensed she did not feel that way in her heart.

Around 2:00 P.M., my phone rang. It was Danielle. I still had a rush of excitement when she called.

"I missed you."

"I finished class early today. Can I stop by?" As if she ever had to ask.

"What time will you be here?"

"I should be there in half an hour.

"See you then."

"Be ready."

I spent the next few minutes straightening up the apartment. I remembered Allison had left a scented candle in the cupboard when she moved out. I lit the candle, and a vanilla smell filled the room.

Forty-five minutes later, there was a knock on the door, and Danielle opened it. I always left it unlocked for her. She threw her purse onto the couch, her car keys jingling as they rolled onto the floor.

Allison threw her arms around me and kissed me deeply. "A candle? What's this for?"

"Something I thought you might like."

"Why are you still dressed?" Quickly, we were both standing in the bedroom naked. She pushed me onto the bed. I was lost in the experience as she rode on top of me.

After we orgasmed together, we lay silently, looking into each other's eyes. Finally, I broke the silence.

"I've had a question for you since we started all of this. That first night in the car, you said we didn't have to worry about using protection. It's never come up since. What's the deal?" The uncertainty had weighed on my mind since we met. I was not ready to be a father.

Danielle pulled the sheets down to her waist and took my hand. She brought it to the scars on her abdomen.

"Remember when you asked me about these?" She rubbed my fingers over her two raised lines on her lower belly. "I had my tubes tied after Kyle was born. I knew I didn't want any more kids, so that's why we don't have to worry about any accidents."

I was relieved to hear that she had no chance of getting pregnant. I was quite content having sex without the risk of making a baby.

"Danielle, there's another thing I've wanted to ask you since you first came over. Why are you here?"

"How existential!"

"I mean, why are you here in my bed? You have a husband and kids. When we first met at the Halloween party, I thought it was just a one-night thing, but it's become so much more for me."

I wanted to understand what motivated Danielle to have an affair, not just out of curiosity, but to gauge where our relationship might be heading. Was she planning to leave her husband or looking for fun on the side?

"I don't feel comfortable talking about this."

"Look, we're together in my bed. I need to know why you're here."

Danielle lay quietly for a few minutes. "I don't want to talk about it. I just want to be here with you."

"If you want us to go on, I need to know." It was an empty threat, but I wanted an answer.

"Fine." She sighed, closing her eyes. "Jeff and I have been having problems since Kyle was born. I had a rough pregnancy, and Jeff was never around. He had just been promoted and was working all the time. I resented him for making me go to my doctor's appointments alone. He was supposed to have a regular schedule but always picked up overtime. When it was time for me to go to the hospital, he was nowhere to be found. Jennifer drove to the hospital and stayed with me when I gave birth to Kyle. Jeff finally showed up a few hours later.

"I was a stay-at-home mom for the first year after Kyle was born. I slept next to the baby while Jeff slept upstairs. Even after Kyle started sleeping through the night, Jeff and I continued to sleep in separate bedrooms, and we've slept in separate bedrooms ever since.

"Our marriage is one of convenience for both of us. I don't know if we ever loved each other, or if we both thought we would never find anyone else. I needed a father for Haley, and he wanted a wife. We're not having sex anymore. We barely even see each other. I suspect he might be having an affair, but I don't care. He can sleep with anyone he wants since he's not sleeping with me." She kissed me on the cheek. "That is why I am here."

"Am I a revenge lay then? To get back at Jeff?"

Danielle sat up, the sheets falling off her. "You're so much different from Jeff. I spent months trying to figure out how to approach you. I wanted to know you better, so that night at the Halloween party, when I saw you on the swing, I took the opportunity and I'm so glad I did."

We lay on our backs, holding hands under the covers. The silence between us was comfortable.

"I have to go in a few minutes. What are your plans for tomorrow?" I didn't want to tell her I was meeting Allison, but I felt compelled to tell her the truth. After all, she had just told me about her relationship with her husband.

"I'm getting together with Allison for coffee." I hoped Danielle would tell me I was crazy to see Allison again, that I should forget about her. I wanted her to tell me that she and I had a future, that she had decided to leave her husband so we could be together.

"Did she call you, or did you call her?"

"She called me to see about getting back together."

"I hope it works out. It was her loss when she left you in the first place." With that, she reached under the covers and took me in her hand. "Do you think we can go again?" This time, I was on top, watching the pleasure in her eyes as I moved slowly inside her.

Danielle left about two hours after she came over. She didn't even flinch when I told her about Allison and me getting together. I wanted her to be jealous of my seeing Allison. If she didn't care that I was meeting my ex-fiancée, did she care about our being together?

As Danielle walked out the door of my apartment, I wondered if I was being used. If so, was it terrible? I was having amazing no strings attached sex with no expectation of a future. There were no flowers, no gifts, no awkward dates. We were two people with an incredible sexual attraction.

I should enjoy my time with Danielle. Whatever happens with Allison will happen. I promised myself that I would let my relationships with Danielle and Allison flow where they may. I took a deep breath, closed my eyes, and repeated the phrase "enjoy the ride" over and over.

I fell asleep for an hour, feeling completely relaxed, and had a dream about my next rendezvous with Danielle.

22

— · —

DECEMBER 20TH

I found a parking space directly in front of Reindeer Brew. Through the large picture window of the coffee shop, I could see Allison sitting at a booth. She looked nervous. She glanced around the cafe, appearing on edge. Allison was extraordinarily confident, so seeing her drumming her fingers and chewing her bottom lip was unusual.

Allison still hadn't noticed me when I slid into the booth across from her. Allison looked at me, then stared down at her coffee cup.

"Do you want anything?" She shook her head.

I slid to the end of the bench, but Allison reached across the table and grabbed my hand. "Adam, sit here for a second." I slid back to the middle. "Before you decide if we should fully get back together, I need to tell you something."

"What's up?"

"You know how I told you I slept with someone else when we were apart..." She let the words hang in the air.

I took a deep breath through my nose and sat back. "Yes."

Allison looked up at me, her eyes a mix of sadness and embarrassment. She had always been so stoic when we were together. "The sex was much better with you." I sensed that, even at twenty-two, she felt shame saying the word "sex" aloud.

"That's good to hear, I guess."

"There's something else." She shifted nervously on the bench and gripped her coffee mug. "The first time I slept with this guy, we were both drinking and didn't use any protection." I thought she was going to tell me that she was pregnant. I would definitely walk out then.

"I caught something." I bit my lip, trying not to laugh. Not that it was funny. The situation was horrifying for her, but a base part of me thought she got what she deserved. "I was treated and now have no symptoms."

Without saying a word, I walked over to the counter. I couldn't reconcile the Allison who had abandoned me months ago with the Allison sitting in front of me. Allison was so frigid with me, so resistant to physical intimacy. As I thought about Allison's hookup, I kicked the wooden counter in anger. It had taken three years before we had sex, and one date before she had sex with someone else. e.

I walked back to the table, where Allison continued to stare into her coffee. "Why did you sleep with him on the first date?"

"I don't want to say it was the alcohol, but that was a lot of it. You know I'm not a big drinker, and I had too much that night. I know it's no excuse for what I did."

"Allison, I'm genuinely surprised. I need to know more about this relationship you had." I felt more like a voyeur than an angry lover.

"I was at a bar with Julia and a few other people from my sorority." I knew that bitch Julia was involved. "I met this guy who had graduated from Duke Med School. I told him I was starting there next year, and we got to talking. We ended up making out in his car and then went back to his apartment." She paused to gauge my reaction. I imagined I was supposed to feel disgusted at my ex-fiancée sleeping with another man, but I was strangely aroused by Allison telling me this story.

"We went to dinner a few more times. Then, he started his ICU rotation and had no time to spend with me. After a few weeks, we never talked again."

I let the silence hang for a minute. "I can try to forgive you, but I can't make any promises." I looked across the table. "There's one thing I never understood. Why does Julia dislike me so much?"

"I wouldn't say she dislikes you. She doesn't think that you and I are the best fit."

"Why not? Am I not good-looking enough for you?"

"No, nothing to do with your looks. Remember, these are her words, not mine. She feels that I am much more driven than you, and you won't be able to keep up with me in life. You're much more emotional than I am, and you have a high sex drive that I can't match. Julia thinks that our marriage will never work."

I sat quietly for a minute, thinking about Julia's words. As much as I hated Julia, maybe she was right.

"Is that why Julia set you up with that guy you slept with?"

"She thought I needed more experience dating before I settled down."

I was pissed. Julia couldn't get her own dating life together, so she lived her romantic life through Allison. Julia aggravated every guy she dated. She loved to pontificate on the state of women's rights and quote authors no one had heard of. I didn't know how anyone could stand her for more than ten minutes.

"You talked about our sex life with Julia?"

"She's my best friend, Adam. Who else would I talk to? I only had you and her, and you were gone. So yes, I talked to her." There was a lull in the conversation as I stared out the window to hide my annoyance. "I missed you, Adam, and I'm glad we're giving this another try."

We stood up and put on our coats. As we walked to the door, she put her arm around mine and leaned her head against my shoulder. "This feels right. I missed you in my life. Thank you for being so accepting."

Allison's nose turned red in the chilly night air. I rubbed it gently. "You'd better get somewhere warm. I'll talk to you soon."

I watched her walk down the street and turn around the corner. I smiled smugly. Allison had come back to me after all. She realized she had made a mistake by walking out on me. I had the upper hand in our relationship for a change, and I planned to use it to my advantage.

23

DECEMBER 22ND

Jennifer and I were working our last scheduled shift before Christmas. We were stationed at the main EMS base on Medic Two. It was Friday afternoon, and the administrative staff had left for the holiday. Unlike our usual weekdays, the base was quiet. The room was decorated with tinsel, and someone had hung mistletoe from the ceiling. The place had a cheap holiday feel.

Jennifer and I sat on the couch watching the local afternoon news. When the show went to commercial, Jennifer surprisingly asked, "How are things going with Danielle?"

I knew Jennifer had given Danielle my phone number after the Halloween party, but I didn't realize she was following our relationship. Jennifer sensed my hesitation to respond. "Don't worry, Adam. I don't tell secrets."

From the way she gossiped around the base, I knew that wasn't true, but I desperately wanted to tell someone about my relationship with Danielle. I wanted someone to know how incredible she felt lying next to me, and I had to find someone who would not judge me for sleeping with a married woman.

Jennifer sensed I wanted to talk. "Danielle and I have known each other for a long time. We went to EMT school together ten years ago, and we've been friends ever since. I know all the shit she's gone through."

We had been partners for five months and had already discussed her dating life ad nauseam. Since I didn't judge her relationships, I hope she would not judge mine.

"Danielle's incredible. Our attraction to each other is unbelievable. The sex is intense. When we're in bed together, the world feels right."

"Do you ever go anywhere?"

I was ashamed when I answered no. It reminded me that all we did was have sex, never any real dating.

"A bit of advice about Danielle. I love that girl with all my heart, but she's poison. You're not the first guy she cheated with, and you won't be the last. She knows that her marriage to Jeff was a mistake, but she doesn't want to be alone. She's willing to stay in a terrible marriage to keep a father for her kids." Jennifer paused. "He's probably cheating too, so don't feel guilty about that. You're not breaking up their marriage."

I felt a stabbing sensation in the left side of my chest that made me hyperventilate. I thought Danielle had chosen me because I made her feel loved and brought her happiness. She told me that she found my intellect attractive. As it turns out, she had chosen me because I was an easy target for her to seduce. My stomach dropped as I realized I was just another in a line of men with whom she was cheating.

But I was different than the men she had been with in the past. She dated a loser in high school and was married to a man who cared little about her. I was a Duke graduate. I would take care of her despite her flaws and imperfections. Her past didn't bother me. I wanted her in my future.

The buzzer in the lounge interrupted my train of thought. "Medic Two, respond to 140 North Roxboro Road for a cardiac arrest." Cardiac arrests were a bread-and-butter call for EMS, but despite what was shown on TV, we rarely brought anybody back. Most patients were older folks who had a slew of medical problems. I found it sad when we had to perform CPR on an eighty-year-old with dementia who could not recognize their family. With each chest compression, we shattered ribs and pierced internal organs. We would try to get the family to allow their loved one to die in peace, but usually, they wanted "everything" done. They expected us to raise the dead, but we were not miracle workers.

We responded to the call with lights and sirens, arriving eight minutes after dispatch. The fire department was already on scene. Jennifer and I grabbed the cardiac monitor, medication bag, and airway equipment and headed into the house. A man and a woman in their fifties sat on the couch, crying. A police officer stood quietly next to them. He motioned for us to go down into the basement.

Jennifer and I descended a rickety wooden staircase. We found four firefighters around the body of a man. A single piece of rope swung from one of the wooden rafters.

The captain gave me a quick report as three firefighters performed CPR. "A twenty-two-year-old male found hanging from the ceiling by his parents. He was last seen about half an hour ago. We cut him down when we got here and started CPR. The defibrillator said no shock advised."

"Thanks, Captain." Jennifer had already begun hooking up our cardiac monitor. I took my place at the head of the patient to insert a breathing tube into the man's lungs. I opened my airway roll, finding the appropriately sized equipment.

"Stop CPR!" I ordered as I studied the monitor. "Asystole." A flat line with no cardiac activity. "Get back on the chest," I told the firefighters as they restarted compressions.

As I prepared to place the breathing tube, I got a closer look at his head. His face was bloated and a dark shade of blue. A large ligature mark encircled his neck circumferentially. His eyes bulged out of his head, a clear sign of suffocation. I shined my penlight in his eyes. His pupils were dilated and did not respond to the light.

"Let's check the rhythm again," I ordered. The firefighters stopped compressions. The monitor still showed a flatline. "Continue CPR. I'm going to call the medical command to see if we can stop the resuscitation." This was not a survivable injury.

I changed the channel on my radio until the digital screen read Duke ED. "Medic Two calling Duke ED for medical command orders." There was a pause.

"Go ahead, Medic Two, this is Doctor Cohen."

"Good evening, Dr. Cohen. This is Paramedic Lawrence on Medic Two calling for field termination."

"Go ahead."

"We were dispatched to a cardiac arrest. Twenty-two-year-old man who hung himself. He was last seen thirty minutes prior to the call. First responders found him pulseless and apneic, with no shock indicated on their defibrillator. He is asystolic on the monitor, and his pupils are fixed and dilated. There is a large ligature mark on his neck. Request field termination."

"Request for field termination is granted." The radio crackled as the doctor signed off.

I looked at my watch. "The time of death will be 4:53 P.M."

Everyone took a deep breath for a few seconds to let the adrenaline wear off. The firefighters were sweating from performing CPR. Even though there was no hope of bringing this man back, everyone had tried their hardest. I paused for a moment of silence. "Thank you, everyone."

Jennifer rolled up the monitor leads and stowed the airway equipment. The firefighters put the bloody medical equipment in a red biohazard bag. It would be my job to tell this man's parents that he had died.

"Do you know his name?" I asked the fire captain. He opened a wallet he had taken from the man's pants. His driver's license read William Carter.

I trudged slowly up the basement steps into the living room, planning what I would say to the family. I had only broken the news of a loved one's death once before. In that case, it was an elderly patient on hospice, so the death was expected. This man, who had taken his own life, was the same age as me.

I was inadequately trained to break this news. In paramedic school, we spent less than an hour discussing death notifications. There were no simulations, no practice, just generic advice to use the word "death" and avoid medical jargon. The topic of breaking bad news deserved much more discussion. It was less stressful to take care of the sickest trauma patient than to break the news of death to a family.

I found William's parents still sitting on the couch. Their arms were wrapped around each other, both sobbing. I suspected they knew what I was about to tell them. After all, they had found their son swinging from a rope in the basement.

"My name is Adam," I said, kneeling in front of the couch. "Are you William's parents?" They nodded, too tearful to say words. "When we found William, he had no pulse and was not breathing. We weren't able to get his heart restarted, and he died." With that statement, William's parents started wailing. The police officer stood awkwardly beside them, unsure of what to say. He pushed a box of tissues closer to the couple. "I'm very sorry for your loss," I said quietly, but they didn't hear me over their despair.

I kneeled next to the couch, waiting for the appropriate time to get up. The firefighters came up the steps and quietly filed out of the house. Jennifer came up shortly after, carrying our equipment. I took Jennifer's arrival as an opportunity to leave, following her outside. The scene was turned over to the police to await the arrival of the medical examiner.

Jennifer and I put our equipment back into the ambulance. I watched as the fire engine pulled away, although several police cars remained outside the house. The lights on our ambulance flashed red and white. Neighbors stood on their front lawns, speculating about what had happened.

Time froze as I stood outside the ambulance. I gazed at the clear night sky and the millions of stars. I couldn't imagine what it must be like for a parent to lose a child three days before Christmas, especially when that child took his own life. I wondered what demons were harbored in that man's brain—a man exactly my age.

Life could be short and fleeting, whether by suicide, accident, or bad luck. Danielle made me excited to get up every morning. She filled my life, so I was no longer empty. Whatever years I had left, be five or fifty, and I wanted to spend them with Danielle.

Jennifer put her hand on my shoulder. "Ready, Adam?" I nodded, knowing it was time to be available for the next call. I had hoped we wouldn't get one because I was in no state of mind to provide emergency care. I stuffed my sadness into the back of my brain and went back to work, praying for the end of my shift.

24

December 24th

I walked around Allison's attic bedroom for the first time in months. She hoped a visit would prove to her family that I was worth having in her life. I was working Christmas night but had Christmas Eve off, so I planned to drive back to Durham in the morning.

The attic was Allison's bedroom growing up. It was long and narrow. There were two twin beds, one under each side of the slanted roof. At the end of the beds, the room opened up. There was the white desk where Allison had done her schoolwork. Above the desk was a bulletin board with photos of Allison tacked to the cork. Other photos sat in frames on top of a matching white dresser. In all the pictures, she was dressed in figure skating apparel. The photos showed Allison in various settings, some posed, while others captured her in midair, whirling above the ice. There was a picture of her with a gold medal around her neck, holding a dozen red roses.

I picked up a silver oval frame with Allison's senior high school photograph. She wore a high-necked black dress and a simple string of pearls around her neck. Allison had attended an elite private school in Greensboro where her mother taught

English. She otherwise could have never afforded the tuition. Allison never needed to prove herself academically; she graduated as valedictorian of her class. However, her classmates were from the old-money crowd, so she had to prove she was worthy of being part of that social caste.

I picked up another photo off the desk. Allison had her arm around her forever best friend, Aubrey. Aubrey's family came from the Old South. Her family still lived on the tobacco plantation her great-great-grandfather had owned.

Aubrey was the cheeriest person I had ever met, with long brown hair, dimples, and deep hazel eyes. She always smiled as she spoke in a slow Southern drawl. Compared to Allison's intensity, Aubrey was relaxed and charming. I could see how Aubrey would make the perfect wife for a man in the upper crust of North Carolina society. Although she had just graduated from the University of North Carolina with a degree in communications, she never planned to work. For her, the aim of college was to find the perfect husband.

Allison and I attended Aubrey's debutante party during our sophomore year of college. The affair was held at the Red Oak Country Club in a formal dining room with large chandeliers hanging from the glass ceiling. The room overlooked a stunning golf course, a perfectly manicured sea of green extending into the distance. Everything in the room was white: round tables with crisp white linen, every chair covered with white cloth and encircled by a white bow. Each young woman was presented to the crowd by her father. They came forward, clad in a pure white dress, and curtsied while the guests clapped quietly.

After the presentation of the young women, a brass band played swing, jazz, and beach music. The whole Southern debutante concept was foreign to me. I found it pretentious and a waste of money.

As we were expected to dance at the debutante party, Allison's parents had tried to teach us the North Carolina state dance, the shag. I remember the song playing on a turntable: "You're More than a Number in My Little Red Book." I took four steps before I stomped on Allison's feet. What I remember most was the way her father and mother interacted. Effortlessly and without speaking, their bodies moved in sync. Neither of them was a passionate person. I never saw them kiss during the entire time Allison and I were together. But on that night, I saw why their marriage lasted twenty-eight years. They moved in perfect sync: their bodies, their minds, and their souls. I doubted I could ever have that connection with Allison.

I looked around Allison's bedroom. Gold and silver medals hung on the wall, each with a red, white, and blue ribbon. I picked up a medal that had the USA National Team logo on its face. At that moment, I felt utterly inferior to Allison. Medal after medal attested to her skating successes. Her athletic prowess was outshone only by her academic achievements.

I sat at the white desk, imagining Allison studying here as a teenager. I could feel the intensity as Allison poured over Shakespeare and math problems until the early morning.

The stairs creaked as Allison walked into the attic. "What are you doing up here?"

"Just looking at your old stuff." She padded gently across the carpet and kissed me softly on the lips. "The eggnog is ready.

Come down and join us." Although Allison was demonstrably affectionate with me since arriving in Greensboro, it felt forced and unnatural. We kissed on the cheeks, not the lips. If I touched her in any way that might seem sexual, she pulled away. Danielle had changed my outlook on relationships. I needed that sexual chemistry. I couldn't imagine a marriage without it.

Hand in hand, Allison and I went down to the den. In the corner sat a carefully decorated Christmas tree. Tinsel was strung in parallel rows. White ornamental balls hung from the branches. Allison's father sat in a wing-back chair at the far end of the room, across from the entertainment center. An orchestra was playing Christmas songs on the TV. Allison's mother sat bolt upright on the couch with her hands folded in her lap. She wore a long green plaid skirt and a white turtleneck. Faith sat next to her. Her shoulder-length blonde hair was kept in place with a green plaid headband. At Faith's feet sat Pilot, the family's chocolate Labrador retriever.

Pilot was the member of the family I liked most, maybe even better than Allison. He lay quietly on his stomach in front of the couch, his head pressed against the floor. Allison and I sat on the hardwood floor, our backs against the sofa. Pilot's nails scraped the wood floor as he scooted over to Allison, putting his head in her lap. He rolled onto his back and looked up at her, waiting for her to scratch his belly.

Although the whole family loved Pilot, he was Allison's dog. Pilot could sense her mood the minute she walked in from a skating competition. If Allison won, he would jump up and put his paws on her shoulders, hugging her in celebration. But if Pilot sensed Allison had lost, he would follow her up into her room and lie at the foot of the bed while she cried.

We watched the Christmas concert with little conversation. Allison's mother hummed along, tapping her hands gently on her knees. Allison's father sat motionless in his armchair, occasionally smiling at Allison's mother. I felt stifled, as if I were trapped in a wax museum. Allison's family, except for Pilot, ignored me. I was saved by the chocolate lab, who stuck his head in my lap whenever Allison stopped rubbing him.

The concert ended at 10:00 P.M., and we said goodnight. I walked up the two flights of steps into the attic and changed into my pajamas. Even though Allison and I had been dating for four years, she would sleep in her sister's bedroom. Her parents did not approve of cohabitation before marriage. They were dismayed when we moved in together after graduation. They blamed me for pressuring her into living together, not believing it could have been Allison's choice.

I heard Allison's footsteps as she came up into the attic. I was already under the covers. She crawled onto the bed but stayed on top of the covers. She put her nose against mine, smiled, and kissed me on the lips. I slipped my hand under her shirt and rubbed her back. I tried to unhook her bra, but she stood up.

"We can't do this now."

"I've missed you." I pulled her hand to bring her closer.

She kneeled on the floor next to my bed and put her hands in my hair. "I can't do this while my parents are home."

"They're on the first floor. I promise I'll be very quiet."

Allison pulled away again. "Stop! I'll see you in the morning."

Without saying goodnight, she disappeared down the steps. I was alone in the attic bedroom. I felt the chilly air coming through the single-pane window. My mind wandered to Danielle. I stared at the empty twin bed across from me. I pictured Danielle tucked into bed wearing only a long T-shirt. She smiled at me and motioned for me to come closer. I closed my eyes and fell asleep, dreaming about making love to Danielle.

25

— · —

JANUARY 22ND

The plane's tires screeched on the runway as I landed in New Orleans. It had been a brief two-hour flight from Durham. Tomorrow morning, I had an interview at the Tulane School of Medicine. I had already interviewed at Duke and the University of North Carolina. I had no misgivings that both would reject me. My science grades and test scores were mediocre at best. My practical experience in medicine was the one aspect that set me apart from my peers.

I hadn't checked any luggage, so I exited the airport quickly with my garment bag in hand. This was my first time in the Big Easy. As I walked through the terminal, I was greeted by the colors of Mardi Gras: purple, green, and gold. I walked past signs for world-famous restaurants, found the taxi line, and was ushered towards a white and red cab.

"Where to, honey?" the cab driver asked.

"The Hilton on St. Peter's."

The driver eased away from the curb and honked at oncoming traffic. She crossed two lanes of traffic, cutting off a car rental bus.

"Where are you from, honey?" I barely understood the question through her thick Cajun drawl. I looked at her through the rearview mirror. She was a gaunt woman in her fifties with a weathered face from too much time in the Louisiana sun. As she talked, she turned her head towards me, her eyes drifting from the road.

"North Carolina," I replied bluntly.

"I got a sister in Myrtle Beach. You ever been there?"

"Nope." I stared out the window, hoping to avoid further conversation, but the woman kept talking. We passed the Superdome, and she pulled to the curb in front of my hotel.

"Enjoy your stay, baby."

As I climbed out of the cab, I watched a horse clip-clop past on the cobblestone. The equine pulled an open-air carriage filled with a family enjoying the charm of New Orleans. I heard the faint sound of Zydeco music from a nearby club. I strained to hear the accordion playing a bluesy tune accompanied by the staccato of a washboard.

I checked in and rode the elevator to the sixth floor. From my room, I could see the neon lights of the French Quarter. I would be in New Orleans for less than twenty-four hours. I would have time to finish my interviews, tour the hospital, and catch my flight home. Tonight, I wanted to experience the city, eat beignets at Café Du Monde, and walk down Bourbon Street.

I strolled down St. Peter's Street until I reached Canal, the border of the French Quarter. The iron wheels of the street cars screeched down the metal tracks. I watched groups of people walk by, carrying plastic cups of all shapes and sizes filled with alcohol. One cup was shaped like a hand grenade with a long neck, while another woman carried a large yellow plastic cup filled with a hurricane.

When I stepped onto Bourbon Street, the pungent odor of stale beer mixed with urine hit me. Neon signs advertised strip clubs and cheap drinks. I dodged a woman vomiting and squeezed through a crowd of tourists. When I made a right off Bourbon Street, the crowd significantly thinned. I walked past the St. Louis Cathedral, where artists displayed their work on the wrought-iron fence encircling the church. A man spray-painted designs onto T-shirts while another artisan hammered out metal sheets in the shape of the fleur-de-lis.

On my way back to the hotel, I grabbed a shrimp po'boy and an order of beignets. I found a small park surrounded by a high fence with gates at each corner. The gates were open, despite a sign stating that the park closed at dusk. I sat down on a bench and unwrapped my sandwich. Lights at each corner of the park cast a dim glow over the grass. Across the way, I saw an older woman walking two gray miniature poodles. She let them off the leash, and they ran around, sniffing and peeing. One dog jogged over to me, its interest piqued by the smell of my sandwich.

"Coco, come here." The woman waved to me apologetically, and I waved back. I loved dogs, though I never had one growing up. Maybe I would adopt a dog of my own in my next apartment.

I finished my sandwich, enjoying the quietness of the park. Although we were only a five-minute drive from the French Quarter, the area was completely quiet. I reflected on my relationships with Danielle and Allison. I was uncertain which relationship I wanted to prioritize. Could Danielle and I have a future outside of the bedroom? Could Allison and I ever find happiness together?

One of the park gates close with a metallic clang, followed by the sound of a chain being pulled around it.

"Closing time," announced a man. He wore green work clothes and padlocked another entrance to the park.

In Durham, I felt isolated. I had no friends except Allison, and our relationship was uncertain. I'm not sure I could call Danielle a friend, as we only saw each other to have sex. In New Orleans, musicians played jazz on the corner. I could walk down Canal Street to the banks of the Mississippi, people watching, feeling connected to the city. I much preferred the bustle of the city to the isolation of Durham. As I walked back to my hotel, I decided New Orleans could definitely be in my future.

26

— · —

JANUARY 30TH

Jennifer and I were working the night shift out of South Station, an old brick building in downtown Durham. At various times, the building had served as a nursing home, psychiatric hospital, and now as a public health center. Yearly, the city council would propose replacing the building, which had long outlived its useful life, but it would route money elsewhere, allocating just enough money to patch the building together for another year.

We were stationed in a small section of the building near the loading dock. Jennifer and I were kicked back in recliners watching a movie. The EMS room was just as rundown as the rest of the building. Brown water stains dotted the white popcorn ceiling tiles. There was one bunk room, but we rarely used it since we often found roaches crawling around on the floor. The South base was the busiest station in the city, so there was seldom time to sleep anyway.

The buzzer interrupted the movie. A voice boomed through the speaker. "Medic Five, respond to 33 Ontario Street for a subject down." Jennifer and I looked at each other and frowned. The Ontario housing projects were a relic of segregation. The single-story apartments covered six square blocks. They were referred to as garden apartments, but there was no greenery to be seen. We did not go into the projects without a police escort. My coworkers had been assaulted, hit with bottles, or threatened by crowds.

I tied my boots and walked into the cold January night air. Before getting in the ambulance, I put on my black Kevlar vest with silver reflective lettering on the back, identifying me as a paramedic. Ballistic vests were issued to all EMS clinicians, but most wore them only when working at the Southern base. Not only did they protect against bullets, but knives and blunt objects as well. How sad that EMS clinicians needed to dress for a war simply to provide medical care.

"542 to Dispatch," I heard a police officer say on the radio.

"Go ahead, 542."

"I have an approximately twenty-year-old male shot in the head. Have EMS expedite."

I picked up the microphone from the center console. "Medic Five, we copy. Is the scene secure?" Although the address was around the next corner, we would not enter the area without knowing there was no active shooter.

"Scene secure," the police officer responded. "Come around to the back of building F."

Jennifer parked the ambulance in front of a line of police cars. I grabbed the trauma bag out of the side compartment of the ambulance and threw it on the stretcher. Dim orange floodlights shone down from the top of the buildings into the courtyard, but half were burned out. We walked between long shadows and dim spaces. Each apartment had a set of gray concrete steps that led into the back of the house from the courtyard. Trash littered the area: a broken bike here, a crumpled beer can over there. None of the residents of the Ontario projects were out at this time of night. After dark, they fled into the refuge of their apartments.

An officer shone his flashlight on a body lying in front of a green dumpster, the beam fixed on the man's face. The officer was young and appeared to be fresh out of the academy. Jennifer and I lowered the stretcher. I heard more police sirens coming.

A police officer shone his flashlight on a body lying in front of a green dumpster, the beam fixed on the man's face. The young man's face looked ghostly white as a blue tint encircled his lips.

"Jennifer, I have a pulse. Let's get him on the stretcher and get him out of here." There was not much I could do about a gunshot wound to the head. His only chance of survival was rapid transport to the hospital. "Help us move him," I said to the officer. "Grab his shirt." I pinched the skin on his right shoulder and twisted it to evoke a painful response, but there was none.

The officer grabbed the patient's T-shirt while I held his loose-fitting jeans at the waist. Jennifer lifted the legs, and lowered the man onto the stretcher. We moved quickly, maneuvering across the dirt, back to the ambulance. We slid the stretcher into the ambulance and locked it in place.

"What do you need?" Jennifer asked.

"Get me a blood pressure while I strip him." I needed to see if he had any other gun shot wounds that required treatment. In the light, I took a closer look at his face. He wasn't more than sixteen years old. His hair was braided in tight cornrows. He wore a striped sweater and a pair of baggy jeans. I took my trauma shears and cut straight down the front of his shirt, fileting it open. I did the same for his T-shirt underneath. The man's chest had several large tattoos in black script lettering.

As Jennifer kneeled on the floor taking a blood pressure, I slid around to the foot of the stretcher. I cut straight up each pant leg, looking for other wounds, but found none.

"I'm getting 102 systolic."

"Let's get going. Give Duke a heads-up when you can."

A police officer opened the back door of the ambulance. "Which hospital are you going to?"

"Duke! Now close that fucking door!"

Jennifer flipped on the sirens and pulled away from the curb with a squeal. "Medic Five, on our way to Duke with one code three," I heard her say on the radio. The ambulance made several quick turns as we wound our way out of the narrow streets of the Ontario projects.

I felt tunnel vision in the back of the ambulance. The wailing sirens seemed distant. I shined my penlight in his left eye, then in the right. They were dilated with no response from either pupil. During the next few minutes, the patient's breathing slowed. I placed a mask on the man's face and squeezed air into his lungs, but his chest didn't move. Desperately needed oxygen was not reaching his body. The ambulance hit a bump, and I bounced out of the captain's chair, landing on the floor. With the rush to get the patient into the ambulance, I had forgotten to buckle my seat belt. I shook myself off, climbed back in the chair, and clicked the lap belt around my waist.

"How much longer, Jennifer?" I was losing this patient and was powerless to do anything about it.

"About seven minutes! The highway's one lane because of construction."

It was time to place a breathing tube. I opened the roll that contained my airway equipment and placed it on the counter next to me. I took a deep breath and visualized how I would open the airway, place the laryngoscope blade in the mouth, and slide the tube down into the lungs. This would be my first time placing a breathing tube without backup. If only real life was easy as performing the procedure on a plastic mannequin.

I tried to open the patient's mouth, but his teeth were clenched together. There were medications to deal with this problem in the hospital, but we didn't carry those drugs in the ambulance. I put the mask over the patient's face again and squeezed it once every five seconds. I counted in my head: one thousand, two thousand, three thousand, four thousand, breathe. This time, I was able to get chest rise.

The siren yelped and turned off. I saw the illuminated sign for the Duke Emergency Department through the back door of the ambulance. The truck turned quickly to the left and beeped as Jennifer backed into a parking space.

"Ready to move?"

I nodded, squeezing air into the patient as we rolled from the ambulance into the emergency department. The surgical team was already waiting for us in the trauma bay. We pulled our stretcher next to the hospital gurney and quickly transferred the patient.

"Everyone quiet!" yelled Dr. Garcia, one of the new trauma surgeons at Duke. "I want to hear the EMS report." He pointed to his team standing around the bed. "Get all his clothes off!" He turned to me. "You have twenty seconds. Go!"

"Approximately sixteen-year-old male, found down, single gunshot wound to the head. I didn't find any other injuries. I've been assisting his ventilations for the entire ride."

I stepped to the back of the trauma room, watching the treatment unfold. A nurse on each side of the patient placed an IV line. A technician hooked the patient up to the monitor. The physician at the head of the bed called for medications to facilitate placing the breathing tube. The surgical resident yelled out the physical exam. Under the bright hospital lights, brain matter was visible from the wound.

One day, I would no longer be standing in the back of the room. As an emergency physician, I would be at the bedside, placing the breathing tube and asking the questions in the trauma bay. I would have the skills to save this man's life well beyond what I could do as a paramedic.

Dr. Garcia was quiet throughout the initial resuscitation. Now, he took control. "I want to get him intubated right now. After the X-ray, we'll package him up and take him down to CT scan. I want to be out of the trauma bay in seven minutes." He gave them a goal, and he expected them to meet it. Within six minutes, the trauma team was rolling to CT scan. I was sure that the imaging would show he had a non-survivable brain injury. I hoped he might be an organ donor.

When I got back to the ambulance, Jennifer was wiping blood off the stretcher. "Adam, you did a great job on that call." She had never praised me before. Unlike the hospital, where there is a team of specialists taking care of patients, in the field, it was just my partner and me. There was no one else to give you feedback or praise.

"Thanks," I mumbled as I organized the equipment in my airway bag.

As the adrenaline from the call ran out, I felt a sense of sadness. A young kid, no more than sixteen, had been shot in the darkness behind a rundown housing project. If he didn't die, he would be brain-dead.

We never talked about our feelings in EMS. We joked around to avoid displaying our true emotions. We cried on the way home from work to release the terrible things we saw every day.

Jennifer interrupted my thoughts. "All set?"

I stared at her for a minute before answering. I was still trying to process the call. It was much easier to take care of eighty-year-olds who passed away than young people who died a violent death. Old people were supposed to die, the circle of life and all that. This young man's life was just beginning.

I took a deep breath, closed my eyes, and inhaled the chilly night air through my nose. "I'm good." I wasn't good.

Jennifer let the dispatchers know that our medic unit was back in service. There was a minute of silence until the dispatcher's voice came over the radio again. "Medic Five, are you still on the air?" Jennifer acknowledged.

"Medic Five, respond to police headquarters, 100 East Main Street, in the holding area, chest pain."

I sighed and let out a long breath, anticipating a patient looking to get out of jail for a few hours. It was time to stuff my emotions back inside and return to work. The clock read 4:00 A.M. I needed to fake empathy for the next three hours until I could escape to the silence of my apartment.

27

FEBRUARY 14TH

Valentine's Day marked the day Allison and I would officially get back together. This was the day we would restart our life as a couple. Over the last two months, I perseverated about her having sex with someone other than me. I still felt angry and betrayed, but the logical part of me knew I could only hold so much against her since I was sleeping with Danielle at the same time.

Allison and I had seen little of each other since Christmas. I had been traveling for medical school interviews. We had gone on a few dinner dates. We had even fooled around in the car, but we hadn't gone farther. Allison didn't seem ready to jump back into sex, and I was perfectly satisfied with my physical relationship with Danielle.

Allison lived in an apartment complex about ten minutes away from me. I approached Allison's door with ambivalence. Part of me doubted we could ever reconcile. We were very different people, and I couldn't focus on repairing my relationship with Allison while also sleeping with Danielle. Still, I wasn't ready to give Danielle up. She made me feel valued, something still lacking in my relationship with Allison.

When she opened the door, Allison wrapped her arms around me. In all the times we had lived together, she had never greeted me like that. She propped her arms on my shoulders and looked into my eyes. "It's good to have you back. I missed you."

I wanted to say, "I've been here all along. You're the one who left me." I kept my mouth shut, smiled, and kissed her.

Allison saw me looking around her small studio apartment. "I don't get too many visitors. This place will get me through the next six months until school starts."

I could smell fish in the oven. A pot was boiling on the stovetop, and Allison poured in some grains. "Quinoa. I know how much you like it."

As Allison moved around the kitchen, I was reminded of watching her mother cook. She was a prolific chef. Every meal at Allison's house was homemade; eating out was a luxury for her family. Allison's mother took pride in her ability to feed her family every night. She knew how to cook all the usual Southern staples, such as grits and hushpuppies. She also made delicious pies and cobblers from the fruit of the season.

Allison stirred the quinoa while we chatted about my job. She had rarely been interested in my work in the past. While she cooked, I told her about some of my recent calls: a shooting, a car accident, and a sad case of child neglect. On my last shift, we had been called to an apartment for an overdose. The entire apartment smelled like urine, and there was no heat. Even more disturbing, the apartment had one bedroom, but we found mattresses strewn all over the floor. Twenty people must have lived in that apartment meant for three or four. There were at least three cribs in the apartment, along with boxes of diapers and piles of infant clothes.

We asked no questions about the living conditions because there was no one to ask. The residents of the apartment had scattered when we arrived.

Allison pulled a tray of salmon out of the oven and squirted lemon through a cheesecloth onto the fish. She put a plate in front of me and sat on the barstool next to me. Before we ate, she put her hand on my arm. "It's awesome to be sitting here with you again."

I wanted to believe her, but I still had my doubts. Even if Allison wasn't telling the truth about being back together, it was nice to feel her touch. For the first time in a while, I felt Allison wanted me in her life. She was doting on me, and I appreciated it. I couldn't push aside the four years we had spent together.

I took a bite of my salmon. It was cooked perfectly. Allison jumped up and exclaimed, "I almost forgot!" She went to the refrigerator and pulled out a bottle of Chardonnay. She took two small cups from the cupboard, apologizing for not having any wine glasses. Allison raised her glass. "To us and our future."

"I never remember you drinking wine."

"This is for a special occasion." Allison paused. "I know we've talked about everything that happened during our time apart. I can only apologize and tell you I made a mistake." She took another sip of wine and met my eyes. She was looking for forgiveness.

"What have you been doing at work?" I asked. Allison's face brightened up as she talked about testing folks in homeless shelters for HIV. She spoke at a rapid tempo that I had rarely seen. Her passion for her HIV work was something I envied. I did not have that passion for anything in my life.

"Allison, I'm so impressed with your work and amazed that I will be married to such a talented woman." The words "I'm going to be married" echoed in my head. How could I commit to Allison while I was falling in love with Danielle?

We chatted as Allison cleaned up the dishes and scraped the fish off the pan. Allison dropped the metal tray in the sink with a clatter. "Enough with this cleaning." She whispered into my left ear, "Come with me."

Allison led me to the futon, and we kissed. The kissing got heavier. She untucked my t-shirt from my jeans, pushing me back on the couch. I enjoyed her taking the lead. She slipped off her bra, her chest rubbing against mine. Surprisingly, Allison sat up, unsnapped my jeans, and pulled down the zipper. She reached down into my boxers, taking me in her hand. I should have had a physiological response, but nothing happened. I was completely flaccid.

"What's going on down there?" Allison asked playfully.

After a few seconds, she realized I was no longer looking at her. My mind was elsewhere. I tried to will an erection, but nothing happened. She pulled her hand out of my pants and grabbed her shirt to cover her bare chest. "What the fuck is wrong with me?" Tears welled up in her eyes. "What the fuck is wrong with you?"

I lay on the futon, realizing I wasn't the least bit turned on. Allison glared at me, a combination of rage and embarrassment. "I don't know what the fuck I was thinking." She stumbled into the bathroom and slammed the door. I could hear quiet sobbing, but I was emotionally void. I felt neither remorse nor sympathy. On the floor was Allison's bra. I reached down and picked it up. I held it, hoping intimate material would stir my emotions, but I felt nothing.

I sat down next to the bathroom door and ran my hand over the plush carpet. Inside the bathroom, Allison continued to cry. I felt guilty and confused. Why was I no longer attracted to Allison? She was gorgeous and had a perfect body by any standards. Any man would have enjoyed seeing her naked and making love to her.

"Allison," I whispered through the door, "I don't know what happened."

"How fucking stupid was I to think we could be back together?"

"It's not you. Something happened with me."

"Adam, just go. Get out of my apartment."

"Maybe we can try again," I said half-heartedly. I didn't want Allison to think she was unattractive or that she had done something wrong by taking the lead. Six months ago, her initiating sex would have been unthinkable, so tonight was an enormous change, but my mind was on Danielle.

"Adam, just go."

I pulled on my jeans, grabbed my car keys, and shut the door quietly. I wasn't sure if or when Allison and I might speak again, but I knew it wouldn't be soon. We were no longer compatible. The mind-blowing sex with Danielle had spoiled me. I could never replicate that passion with Allison. I knew the intimacy I wanted in a relationship and would take nothing less. It was time to put Allison behind me and secure my future with Danielle.

28

—·—

FEBRUARY 20TH

I pulled into the parking lot of a local strip mall to get lunch for Danielle and me. I was meeting her at the Roxboro Fire Department, an EMS station in the far north of Durham County. The fire department served an extremely rural area. Although the volume averaged under five hundred calls per year, the station was so remote that it needed to be staffed around the clock. Roxboro was challenging because the nearest hospital was over thirty minutes away. In the city, we could always call the fire department or another ambulance for help. At Roxboro, it was you and your EMT partner. There was no other help coming.

I bolted through the rain, passing a laundromat and an empty store front. At a sandwich shop, I bought an Italian sub for Danielle and a cheese sub for myself. As I drove towards the Roxboro station, the rain became heavier. In the distance, I could see the occasional bolt of lightning flash across the sky. The wipers squeaked harshly along my windshield. After forty-five minutes, I saw a yellow sign marked with a black fire truck. Further along, a single flashing yellow light swung in the wind.

I made a right into the gravel driveway and parked next to Danielle's minivan. Only one other car was in the parking lot, which I imagined belonged to her EMT partner. I took the two sandwiches off the front seat and covered my head as I ran through the downpour. I tapped a code on the electronic keyboard next to the door. The lock clicked open, and I stepped into the crew lounge.

The television was tuned to a reality police show, but the volume was muted. I heard rumbling snores from the recliner, though I could only see a bald head over the top of the chair. There would be a pause before a gasping breath, followed by a sound that was a cross between a bear's growl and an elephant's trumpet.

I took the staircase up to the second floor. There were administrative offices for the fire department and a door with a black nameplate that read "EMS." I stood in front of the door intending to knock, but I knew only Danielle would be in the room.

I opened the door softly. The room, as large as it was, was fairly empty. There were two black leather couches, well-worn but without tears. Caddy-corner from the couches was a large screen projection TV, the type that had become obsolete years ago. No one was motivated to move the behemoth of a television down the steps.

Danielle was asleep on the couch, a hospital blanket covering the lower half of her body. She wore a navy blue T-shirt with the Piedmont EMS logo. She let out an occasional purring snore that I had come to love. I watched her from the doorway, and a feeling of warmth washed over me. I could now definitely say I was in love with this woman.

I kneeled on the floor next to Danielle. She looked so relaxed. I touched her left cheek with the back of my hand. Her facial muscles twitched. Slowly, she opened her eyes. I leaned over and kissed her softly on the lips.

Danielle smiled back at me. "I'm glad you came up to visit. It's been a while, and I was afraid I wouldn't see you this week."

It had been three weeks since Danielle and I had last met at my apartment. "What have you been up to?" I stroked her cheek, enjoying the softness of her skin.

"Stuff." The tone of her voice suggested I should drop the subject.

"What kind of stuff?"

She looked up at the ceiling momentarily, then turned back to me. "I told you before: don't ask questions you don't want to know the answer to."

"Danielle, I want to know what's happening in your life. I hope that one day, we can be..." I trailed off.

Danielle sighed. "Lots of family stuff. Jeff was away at an EMS conference for a couple of nights. I was home with Kyle during the day. Haley had a few soccer games." I turned away and leaned against the couch. Danielle ran her hands through my hair. "Adam, I don't want to worry about these things when I'm with you. You bring happiness and excitement to my life. That's what I love about us."

I stared across the room, feeling her fingernails scratch against my scalp. It made me tingle throughout my body. "Danielle, do you think we have a future together? You're amazing. I want this to be more than just a short-term fling."

Danielle put her finger over my mouth. "I can't talk about this right now."

"You can't tell me you're this passionate with your husband."

"Shut up." She pulled me closer.

"Are you sure we can do this here? We won't get caught?"

"There's no one else in the station, just Rick downstairs. How loud was he snoring when you came in?"

"Loud."

"Then we have nothing to worry about."

"What about lunch?"

"We'll get to it later." She smiled as she pulled me on top of her. "Right now, you are what I need." We made love on the couch, excited by sex in a forbidden place. She came twice, holding a pillow against her face to stifle her screams.

Danielle cleaned herself up with the sheet that had been covering the couch. She put her shirt and uniform pants back on.

"Adam, that was fucking amazing. You feel so good inside me." She kissed me on the lips. "Where are those sandwiches? I am starving after all that."

We sat on opposite couches, eating our hoagies. Our eyes met while our mouths were filled with food. My stomach swirled with nervousness. Now was the time to say it.

"Danielle, I love you."

"Adam, you don't mean that. I am nothing to fall in love with."

"Danielle, I have completely fallen for you. I want you in every way: in my life, in my future, and in my bed."

"Adam, I've fallen for you too." She never used the word "love," but I would take it. Danielle wanted to be with me. Now that I knew how she felt about me, nothing would stand in the way of us.

29

MARCH 3RD

I pulled into a parking space in front of the clubhouse of my apartment complex. I left the car running since I was only grabbing my mail. I pulled three envelopes from the silver mailbox: a water bill, a political solicitation, and a hand-addressed letter from Tulane University. I had only interviewed at Tulane a few weeks ago and wasn't expecting to get a rejection letter so quickly. I thought they would at least put me on the waiting list.

Sitting in my car, I tore open the envelope, leaving the top edge ragged.

"Dear Mr. Lawrence: Thank you for interviewing for the Tulane University School of Medicine. The committee was impressed with your dedication to prehospital care, and the recommendations from your supervisors spoke to your potential as a doctor. After careful consideration, we are pleased to offer you admission...." I skimmed the rest of the letter. "We hope to see you as a student here in the fall." I had been accepted into medical school. I rechecked the letter to ensure I hadn't misread the words. No mistake. I was going to be a doctor.

Sitting in front of the clubhouse, I called my mom to tell her about my admission to Tulane. My mom gushed, telling me how proud she was of my achievement. She filled me in on what was happening in her life and told me stories about my grandmother living in New York. I was isolated from my family, living in North Carolina. Everyone else lived in the Northeast. At most, I would see them twice a year when I flew up for holidays, but I rarely talked to them on the phone.

While she talked, I thought about texting Allison to tell her about my acceptance. I wanted to show her that I was just as successful as her. I was going to be a doctor, just like her. Instead, I located Danielle's number in my contacts. I didn't know how my medical school acceptance would affect our relationship, but I knew she would be excited for me. Danielle had been my biggest supporter through the ups and downs of my applications. Each time I doubted I would ever get into medical school, Danielle reiterated what a great doctor I would be. Now that I had an acceptance in hand, I did not want to lose her by moving away.

"Adam, are you still there?" my mom asked when I didn't respond immediately to her question.

"Sorry, I'm here." I wanted to get off the phone so I could text Danielle. "I want to call Dad before it gets too late."

"I'm so proud of you, Adam, for all your hard work. I love you."

I hung up and texted Danielle. "Call me when you can. I have exciting news!" After ten minutes, nothing came through, so I called my father. I told him about my acceptance to Tulane. He congratulated me and quickly moved on to discussing Yankees baseball. When we finished talking, it was nearly 9:30 P.M. Though I knew he loved me, there was no warmth in our conversations. We said goodbye and promised to speak soon.

I got ready for bed, checking my phone every five minutes, hoping to hear from Danielle. She was the person with whom I most wanted to share my acceptance to medical school. I took a chance and sent one more text. Before I fell asleep, I glanced at my phone, but Danielle still had not responded.

Closing my eyes, I imagined Danielle and I starting a new life in New Orleans. We would have our own apartment and fall asleep next to each other every night. Her kids could come with us. I would Danielle and give her happiness and security. Our life together would be amazing, finally having the freedom to be with each other. I fell asleep knowing, in four years, I would be a doctor.

30

— · —

MARCH 7TH

I pulled into the main EMS station just before 4:00 P.M. for my plum assignment: the University of North Carolina versus Duke basketball game, the final matchup of the regular season. Both basketball teams were perpetually top-ranked, so the UNC vs. Duke game always had the air of a national championship. The rivalry between these two teams, located less than twenty miles from each other, ranked as high as any rivalry in sports.

Although the University of North Carolina had moved into a modern arena in the 1980s, Duke still played in Cameron Indoor Stadium, a small arena built in 1940. The stadium held just over nine thousand fans, including students who packed shoulder to shoulder into the standing-room-only bleachers. A ticket to any Duke basketball game was coveted, but a ticket to a Duke versus North Carolina game would sell for thousands of dollars.

As a student, I never went to a Duke basketball game. For the most popular games, students camped for weeks in Krzyzewskiville, a tent city named after Duke's legendary basketball coach. I hated camping and certainly would not do so for admission to a basketball game. I preferred watching the basketball games from my dorm's common room, where I could eat, drink, and enjoy my space.

Today, I would make up for all those missed games. Two ambulances were assigned to every Duke basketball home game: one for the fans and one for the players. The coveted assignment was the ambulance assigned to the arena floor. Usually, this went to the most senior paramedic. Because this was the last game I would be working as a paramedic for Piedmont EMS, I convinced my supervisor to give me the floor assignment. It also helped that the paramedic on the other truck cared little about basketball. He was much happier napping in the ambulance with his feet on the dashboard.

Jennifer and I drove the few miles from the main EMS base to Cameron Indoor Stadium. It was a beautiful March evening, and the weather was warming up. We drove through East Campus, and I looked at the quad where Allison and I had spent many late nights talking. We drove past the Duke Chapel, and I remembered the spring day a year ago when we got engaged.

Jennifer parked next to the arena entrance. We had eight minutes before we needed to go inside. Hundreds of students lined up to get their spots on the rickety bleachers. Everyone was wearing white or blue face paint. I watched one girl spray blue coloring into another girl's hair. They were laughing, some mildly intoxicated but exuding an overwhelming sense of school spirit.

Jennifer and I piled all our equipment on top of the stretcher. We nodded to a security guard as we pushed the gurney past the locker rooms. The concrete hallway was dim but opened into the brightly lit arena. My heart raced at the excitement of being in the stadium: the squeaking of sneakers on the waxed floor, the fans cheering, and the video screen playing highlights of the Duke season. Adrenaline pulsed through the arena. The Duke pep band was blasting music from their brass instruments. When the music stopped, all the fans, including me, shouted in unison, "Go Duke! Go Duke Go!"

31

— · —

MARCH 15TH

I had not heard from Danielle since our rendezvous at the Roxboro Fire Station. I broke tradition and recklessly called her, but it went straight to voicemail. I even tried phoning the station once when she was working, but she was out on a call. I didn't give my name, and I didn't call back. As far as I knew, we had kept our relationship a secret from everyone except Jennifer. Despite my trepidation that she would talk about Danielle and me, she had kept silent.

In a little over four months, I would leave for New Orleans to become a doctor. Danielle had become so entrenched in my life that I could not imagine a future without her. I wanted Danielle to come to New Orleans with me. She could bring her kids. In four years, I would have a job as a physician that could support us all. I could give her a better life than she had with her husband. She would have money, love, and all the happiness that she deserved.

I couldn't figure out why Danielle wasn't calling me back. As far as I knew, she wasn't busy with school. Usually, she would send a quick text to acknowledge that she couldn't talk. I was frustrated because I knew I couldn't keep calling and texting her. In a regular relationship, I could leave a voicemail or drop by to say hello. At this point, we couldn't risk Danielle's husband finding out, at least not until we finalized our plans for New Orleans. She needed to know I was the man who would care for her and provide for her. We had a future together, and it ran through New Orleans.

32

APRIL 2ND

The alarm in the crew room buzzed. "Medic Six, respond to One Industrial Way, King's Run Motel, for a cardiac arrest."

I marked us responding on the ambulance's laptop. An automated notification popped up on the screen: "Female not breathing, possible overdose." The computer screen displayed a map with turn-by-turn directions, not that we needed them.

The King's Run Motel was one of the most infamous buildings in the city. Once an upscale hotel that served travelers passing through Durham, it was now the most downtrodden lodging in the city. Rarely did a week go by without a major drug or prostitution arrest at the hotel. A few times a year, a dead body was found in the building. Neighborhood residents had tried for years to have it condemned as a public nuisance, but the owners had somehow dodged the local government.

Wayne climbed into the passenger's seat and mumbled, "Let's go."

At 2:30 A.M., there was no reason to use lights and sirens as there were no other cars on the road. Seven minutes later, we arrived at the King's Run. A bright neon sign extending thirty feet in the air announced a rate of forty-three dollars per night. "Ask about our hourly rates," read a smaller sign underneath.

The ambulance bounced through the poorly paved parking lot filled with cracks and holes. We stopped in front of the lobby, parking under a metal awning, which tilted awkwardly to its left, making it appear it could collapse at any moment.

A black and white Durham police car pulled up behind us, and veteran patrol officer Christina Ramirez stepped out. Those who encountered Officer Ramirez underestimated her. She stood five feet four, her jet-black hair pulled back tightly in a bun. Her uniform masked her solid muscles. I had personally watched her take down suspects twice her size with ease. She was a third-degree black belt and had once appeared on a warrior TV reality show.

"I thought I would check in on you guys. Not much going on tonight." She twirled her key ring on her finger and then clipped it on her duty belt in one smooth motion.

We rolled the stretcher up to the glass lobby doors, expecting them to open, but they remained shut. The glass was fogged, and I could see the outline of a man in a chair behind a counter. I banged on the glass, but he did not stir. Christina pulled her expandable baton out of her belt and opened it with a flick of her wrist. I thought she was going to shatter the glass with the metal stick, but instead, she pounded it twice against the metal door frame. The man behind the counter awoke with a start and fell off his chair.

"Hey, dickhead," Officer Ramirez yelled through the door. "We have a medical emergency inside."

With no particular speed, the man sauntered over and flipped a switch above the frame. The sliding glass doors zipped open.

"Where are we going?" I asked the clerk.

"I have no idea." He shrugged and walked back to his desk.

"Medic Six to dispatch. Do you have a room number?"

"The caller stated the second-floor hallway. No further. The call back went unanswered."

I glanced around the sparse lobby. The owners seemed unconcerned about providing a luxurious experience for their guests. A rack of brochures sat half-empty next to the entrance. A few anemic trees dotted the lobby, still living in their plastic pots. Dead brown leaves littered the floor, waiting to be swept up.

When the elevator reached the second floor, it was easy to locate our patient. Down the hall with its dank moist carpet, I could see a figure propped up against the wall, her legs sticking out at an awkward angle. Officer Ramirez yelled down the hall at no one in particular, "Does anyone know who this woman is? Does anyone know where she came from?" The few cracked doors closed at the sight of a police officer.

Our patient leaned awkwardly to her right, her chin tucked into her chest. Scraggly light blonde hair covered her face. She wore ripped jeans with holes in both knees and a light blue tank top covered with stains. I could see the needle marks tracking up and down her arms, a mosaic of her addiction.

I buried my knuckles into her chest, rubbing hard. "Hey! Can you hear me?" She fell onto her side. I grabbed her feet, Wayne grabbed her from under her arms, and we laid her in the middle of the hallway. Her hair fell out of the way, revealing the ghostly white color of her face. There was a blue tinge around her lips. I watched her breathe. Her chest barely rose.

Wayne pulled back her eyelids and shined a light back and forth. "Pupils are pinpoint and non-reactive."

Wayne and I dealt with opioid overdoses regularly, so we both knew what to do. He kneeled at her head and used a resuscitator to squeeze air into her lungs. Within a few breaths, her skin pinked up, and the blueness around her mouth faded.

From my medication bag, I took out a small tan box labeled "naloxone," the antidote for opioid overdoses. I attached the medication to an atomizer to spray the naloxone directly into the patient's nose.

"Ready to raise the dead?" I placed the atomizer into her left nostril and pushed the plunger on the syringe. I stepped back, waiting for the naloxone to kick in. It would take about a minute to reach the girl's brain and restart her breathing.

Slowly, the girl's eyelids flickered. She took a deep breath and sat straight up as if she had awoken from a nightmare. She looked around the hallway, then at me, then at Wayne, utterly unaware of the past few minutes.

"What the fuck happened?"

"You overdosed."

"What are you talking about?" She looked incredulous. "I don't use drugs."

"What's your name?"

"Melissa."

"Melissa, you're not in trouble, but let's not play games with each other. When we got here, you weren't breathing, and your pupils were tiny. We Narcan'd you, and you woke up."

"I'm not going to the fucking hospital!"

"Why not?"

"I'm fine now."

"Melissa, I'm worried that once the Narcan wears off, you could stop breathing again."

She pushed herself back against the wall. She was despondent. Her eyes were empty. She saw no hope in her life. I hoped this was her rock bottom and she was ready for recovery.

"If you don't want to go to the hospital, I can't make you, but I think it would be a really good idea." She didn't answer. "Let us at least check your vital signs." Wayne attached a sensor to her finger to measure her oxygen level and heart rate. He wrapped a blood pressure cuff around her arm.

"Do you have any medical problems like asthma or diabetes?"

"I'm a fucking drug addict."

Wayne finished checking her vital signs; all were within normal limits. "Are you sure I can't convince you to go to the hospital?" She shook her head. "Then I have a piece of paper for you to sign. We offered you a ride to the hospital, and you chose not to go."

Wayne pulled a metal clipboard out of the bag and found a refusal form. He handed Melissa a pen, and she scribbled a signature on the paper.

"Call us back if you need us," I said. It was a formality because we didn't want to come back, and they never called us back anyway. I watched Melissa stand up, holding onto the wall. She stumbled down the hallway and into a room.

We pushed the stretcher back into the elevator. As the door slid closed, Wayne commented wryly, "Another life saved, huh?" I had already seen too many Melissas in my first year as a paramedic. I had resuscitated at least three overdoses at the motel in the last month, not to mention the many patients who received naloxone before the ambulance arrived. It seemed like we were swimming upstream in a river of fentanyl.

Maybe as a physician, I could help patients like Melissa. When they came into the ED, I could provide them with resources for their addiction and medications to ease their pain. I would have time to talk with them in a clean, quiet space, rather than on the nasty floor of a rundown motel.

For now, as a paramedic, offering a ride to the hospital was the best I could do. I left the motel dejected, wondering if we could ever help patients like Melissa.

33

— · —

APRIL 19TH

At noon, my phone buzzed on the nightstand. I struggled to keep my eyes open. I had worked the overnight and it had been busy. There had been several shootings, stabbings, and then retaliatory shootings that kept my truck going the entire shift.

"Hello?"

"Hey, babe. I'm so sorry that I've been out of touch. I know you've been trying to reach me. My daughter had appendicitis, and I was in the hospital with her. There were so many times when I wanted to step out of the room and call or shoot you a text, but I was always worried that she would see my phone."

Over the past three weeks of not hearing from Danielle, I obsessively checked my text messages. I wanted to know that she was thinking of me. I would wake up in the middle of the night to see if she had messaged. I checked my texts first thing in the morning, and as the last thing before I closed my eyes. I was so glad Danielle hadn't forgotten me.

"Adam, I want to see you so fucking badly. I need to feel you inside me. Can I come by around three?"

"I want to see you more than anything."

"Your text said that you had something you wanted to tell me?"

"I'll tell you when you get here."

"I can't wait to hear it." Danielle kissed me through the phone. "See you in a couple of hours. Adam, be ready because I am about to fucking explode."

I fell back asleep; anything to speed up these next few hours until I was inside Danielle.

34

—— • ——

APRIL 19TH

J ust after 3:15 P.M., there was a knock on the door. I stumbled
out of the bedroom, dressed in shorts and no shirt. The extra
few hours of sleep had not cleared my head. I opened the door,
and Danielle stepped inside. She ran her hands over my chest and
through my hair.

"I love this look, Adam. I can touch every inch of your chest."
She ran her hands under my boxers, teasing my erection.

I went to kiss her, but she gently pushed me over the back of the
couch. With a grunt, I flopped onto the cushions, and she kneeled
over me on all fours. She kissed me. I went to kiss her back, but
she playfully pulled her head back up. "What is this big news you
wanted to tell me?"

I tried to sit up and kiss her, but she sat on my waist, pushing her
hips down on mine. She took off her shirt and sat over me in a red
lacy bra. I loved this look, a woman in a bra and jeans. I reached up
to touch her chest, but she waved me off with her pointer finger.
"None of this," she said, running her hands over her breasts, "until
I hear your news."

"I got into medical school!" Of all the people in my life, Danielle
was the one I wanted to tell the most. She smiled and wrapped

her arms around me. Until now, all of our physical contact had revolved around sex. This felt different. This felt like a hug you would give someone you truly had intimacy with.

"Congratulations, Adam, I knew you would do it. Where are you going?"

"Tulane in New Orleans."

"When are you moving down there?"

"At the beginning of August." There was silence between us. I sensed we had two different conceptions of how the next three months would go.

I looked Danielle in the eyes. "I want you to come with me to New Orleans. We can start a life together. I will give you everything you deserve."

"Adam, I know you've thought hard about this, but it would never work."

"Why not? You can work as a nurse, and I can work part-time as a paramedic while I'm in school. We can live simply until I graduate. After that, I will have a decent salary as a resident and then make great money as an attending. I can give you a better life."

"Adam, I've told you over and over that I won't leave my husband. This is my life."

"Bring your kids. We'll find a place big enough for all of us."

"Adam, are you listening to yourself? In what world would that work? I have my life, and you have yours. You can't be a dad to my children when you are barely older than my daughter."

"I'm sure there are other med students with families. We can get married as soon as you're divorced."

"Adam, no! My life is here in North Carolina. It is what it is. My husband is who he is. Nothing is going to change that. These last few months have been an amazing distraction from that life, but it's been just that, a distraction. When it's over, I'm left with my old life. Your future's in New Orleans."

"Our life can be together. It can be what you deserve."

"Adam, maybe I do deserve better. Maybe I'm selling myself short, but reality doesn't bend to people's wishes. I'm not going to move. We can enjoy the next few months until you leave, or we can end it today. What happens is your choice from here, but I don't want to hear about us past August."

"Danielle..."

"Enough! You choose what you want!" Danielle angrily put on her T-shirt, facing away from me. Without another word, she took her keys off the table and slammed the door behind her.

I hyperventilated, feeling my toes and fingers tingle. I pressed my face into the couch cushions, panicking at the thought of losing Danielle. She was the one person in my life who made me happy. The idea of never seeing her again felt like the weight of the sky was crushing me. I had three months to convince her that her future was with me in New Orleans, and I planned to make her see that fact. I could not and would not let her go.

35

— . —

MAY 16TH

Jennifer and I were relaxing on the couches at Girard Station. It had been three weeks since Danielle and I had argued about moving to New Orleans. I knew what I wanted: for us to start a new life together in the Big Easy. The desire I felt for Danielle was stronger than any feeling I ever had for Allison. By comparison, Allison left me flat and numb. When Danielle and I touched, the feeling was intense. I had fallen in love with Danielle, and I had fallen hard.

For now, I would give Danielle what she wanted, to back off any discussion of our future together. I would focus on making our relationship the best it could be. I would do some boyfriend stuff: cook dinner and bring flowers. Maybe I could change her mind if I showed her how much I loved her.

Jennifer broke the silence. "Congrats on getting into med school, Adam. I knew you would make it." How did she know about my acceptance? "Danielle told me," I was annoyed that Danielle had leaked my secret. At some point, I needed to turn in my resignation and announce my move, but I planned to wait at least another month. I did not want my coworkers to treat me differently, knowing I was moving on to medical school.

"How are things going with Danielle?"

"The sex is incredible."

"How about the rest of the relationship?"

"Did she tell you I want her to move to New Orleans with me?"

"Yup."

"And...?"

"You know that's a bad idea, right? You are going to start a new life in a new city. You will finally break free of this place. Danielle will only hold you back. She has kids and a husband. Is that the baggage you want? Seriously, do you want to tell a sixteen-year-old to do her homework? For real? Dude, let her go."

I chewed on my bottom lip, thinking about Jennifer's advice. In some ways, I knew she was right. I should enjoy my time with Danielle for the next few months and start medical school with a clean slate. Leaving Danielle was not easy. I had fallen in love with how her head felt on my chest as I stroked her hair. I had fallen in love with her walking around my apartment wearing only my T-shirt. I had fallen in love with how my pillows smelled after she left.

"Jennifer, there's only one problem. I've fallen in love with Danielle."

"Love, huh? Maybe. Maybe she loves you too." Jennifer made air quotes. "You and Danielle cannot exist in the real world. You are two different people in two distinct stages of your life. This will not end well for either one of you."

"How can love be bad?" I was annoyed with Jennifer. She should have encouraged her best friend to be with the man who would love and care for her.

"Adam, Danielle is one of my best friends, and you're a good friend, too. I would love nothing more than to see you both happy, but I promise you, you will not be happy together. I'll leave you with one more question to ponder: What exactly do you love about Danielle? It seems that what you like is the physical stuff, nothing of substance."

I walked into the bunk room and sat on the bed, separating myself from Jennifer before I lashed out. What did she know about love? For Jennifer, a long relationship meant seeing a guy for more than two dates.

I texted Danielle. "I've been thinking about what you said. I want us to enjoy our next few months together. I can't wait to feel your body against mine."

About fifteen minutes later, I felt my phone vibrate in my lap. Danielle had sent me three kiss emojis. I would use the next few months to show Danielle that her future was with me and prove Jennifer wrong. Danielle and I could be happy together despite the baggage she carried. Love would triumph.

36

MAY 17TH

Through the slits in the vertical blinds, I could see the bright blue North Carolina sky. Wispy clouds floated by. Although it was warm enough to swim, the pool at the apartment complex did not open until Memorial Day. I thought about a hike at the Eno River, but the park reminded me too much of Allison. I was surprised when my phone rang at 9:00 A.M., and I saw Danielle's number on my caller ID.

"Awake?"

"Not quite."

"Do you want to meet up today?" It was unusual for Danielle to call me on the weekend when she usually spent time with her family.

"Of course I want to see you." I hadn't seen Danielle for a week, and I missed the feel of her skin. "When do you want to come down?"

"I can't make it to Durham. Can you come to me around noon?" I was surprised at the suggestion, as Danielle never wanted me to come near her real life. "Jeff is taking the kids to his parents for the day, so I'll be alone."

"Twelve is no problem."

"Meet me in the parking lot of McLean's Store. It's at the corner of Route 42 and Granville Road." She paused. "I can't wait to see you. I think I have a surprise you will very much enjoy."

I showered and shaved, wanting to look good for Danielle. I left around 11:15 AM, wanting all the time I could spend with her. Twenty-five minutes later, I turned off the highway onto a four-lane road. I drove past a strip mall and a few chain drugstores. As I drove farther into the country, open fields replaced commercial buildings. Route 42 turned into a two-lane road as it meandered through farmland. On my right, horses grazed freely in a pasture. To my left, I saw a large barn with peeling red paint.

I put both front windows down, letting the clean country air flow through the car. The radio became increasingly fuzzy, crackling to find a clear signal. I was hypnotized by the undulating green pastures. I rolled up to a four-way yellow flashing light. It was suspended across the intersection, watching like a cyclops over the area. Across the intersection stood a white clapboard building with a faded sign hanging over the front door. I could barely make out the words "McLean's Market" above the Pepsi logo.

I parked and tried to open the store's wobbly front door with faded green paint. It was locked. Through the window, I could see the fluorescent lights of the beverage cases and a deli counter containing rows of meat. Apparently, the market was closed on the weekends.

Across the street was an open field ringed by a row of lemon trees. I could smell the sweet scent in the air and took note of the peacefulness of the countryside. It was a tranquility I had never known growing up. Although I had lived in a sleepy suburb, it was never quiet. There was always noise, whether it was children yelling, a car going by on the street, or church bells in the distance.

Danielle's light blue minivan pulled into the gravel lot and parked next to me. I met her behind her van and kissed her deeply. "I missed you."

I put my hand behind her neck and pulled her towards me. "Not as much as I missed you."

"Come with me," she said, her eyes mischievous. She took a few steps backward and held her right pointer finger in front of her face, motioning for me to follow. She smiled and teased me with her lips. Taking a large flannel blanket out of her van, she led me across the street.

We climbed through the wooden fence and stepped through the densely packed lemon trees. There were no houses or structures on the property, only a vast green meadow with dandelions scattered across the grass. Danielle spread the blanket on the ground. She pushed me down, and I fell with a soft thud onto my back. Birds were chirping in the tree above us. A pick-up truck roared by.

"Don't worry, no one can see us here." Danielle pulled her tank top over her head. She was not wearing a bra. Her pointy nipples stuck out from her small, perky breasts. She pulled off her jeans, revealing the red thong that I loved. Danielle pulled my shirt off, followed by my shorts. I squirmed as she pulled my socks off, inadvertently tickling my feet.

Danielle stroked my hair as I kissed her breasts. She climbed on top of me. I put my hands on her waist as she moved her hips clockwise with me inside her. I looked up at Danielle with love, infatuation, and downright pleasure. I stroked my hands over her body, her back, and her legs, enjoying the feel of her soft skin.

There was complete sexual freedom, making love in a wide-open field under a clear blue sky.

I closed my eyes and moved in rhythm with Danielle. She became increasingly verbal, moaning loudly. There was no reason to stifle her screams.

Suddenly, I heard a high-pitched beep from across the field. A green tractor rolled towards us. As it drew closer, I saw the weathered face of a man, shaded by a baseball cap, with a cigarette dangling from his mouth. Danielle rolled off of me and folded the blanket around us like a burrito.

As the man drove by, he waved nonchalantly at us. "Y'all finish up and clean up when you're done." He made a U-turn and headed back across the field.

Danielle let the blanket go, and we lay naked on our backs, her head in the crook of my shoulder. We both laughed, embarrassed at being seen but also aroused by being caught.

"You heard the man. Let's finish up." I rolled on top of Danielle and looked deep into her eyes as we made love. She breathed quicker and shallower as she neared climax. We were in no hurry, and when we were both ready, we orgasmed together.

We lay for a few more minutes, staring into the blue sky. Danielle had curled her head on my chest. Our breathing became synchronized. The warmth of the sun surrounded us. Lying naked in a field with Danielle seemed completely normal. I closed my eyes, wanting this afternoon never to end.

The thought of staying in Durham for another crossed my mind. I could defer my medical school admission for a year. Maybe Danielle needed extra time to unravel her life so she could come with me. We could be together in North Carolina without the time pressure of leaving in three months. Then we could walk into our new life in Louisiana together.

"You never disappoint me, Adam." Danielle stood up and brushed the grass off her butt. The sun showed from behind her, creating a black silhouette of her against the blue sky. Maybe Danielle's body wasn't quite as perfect as Allison's, but Allison would have never made love completely naked in a field. In four years, Allison never made me feel this good.

After we both dressed, she kissed me on the lips. "So fucking good, Adam." We folded the blanket and ducked through the fence, crossing the street to where we parked our cars. I walked Danielle back to her minivan. She opened the trunk and threw the blanket inside.

I moved toward Danielle, putting my hands around her back. I didn't want her to leave. Danielle gently pulled away, but I held onto her waist.

"Please don't go," I said, feeling a tear pool in the corner of my eye and sniffing.

She touched her pointer finger to my lips. "I have to go. Talk to you soon."

I stood frozen as she climbed into her minivan. She blew me a kiss through the window and backed out of the parking spot, leaving me in a white cloud of dust.

I wanted to be the one that Danielle came home to at night. I wanted to be the one with whom she did yardwork on a Sunday afternoon. Should I go after her right now? Her husband and kids weren't at home. I should tell her exactly how I feel and what I want for our future. I paced around the parking lot, planning my next move. Home or Danielle's house? I chewed my bottom lip. Would she hate me for following her or love me for pursuing her?

I didn't have Danielle's address, but I was sure I could find it online. I searched for her address on my phone. Several potential matches came up, but the addresses were blocked behind a paywall. An hour had passed, and I still hadn't found the information I was searching for.

I set my GPS to take me to my apartment and started the lonely drive back. Tomorrow, I would find her address to see exactly what her life was like. I would convince her that I was the man she should spend the rest of her life with. Danielle was too special to let go of. I knew Danielle felt the same passion towards me. I knew she wanted to be with me just as much as I craved her. Now, we needed a strategy to get out of Durham and go to New Orleans together. Then, our lives would be filled with the love and intimacy we both deserved.

37

MAY 18TH

I woke up the next morning with one mission in mind: to find out about Danielle's life. I needed to know what was missing in her marriage so I could convince her to move to New Orleans with me.

I searched for Danielle's telephone number in a reverse directory but couldn't find her address. Then I searched for her husband, Jeff. A row of images popped up on the screen. I clicked the first photo, which showed a balding man in a white paramedic uniform. There he was.

I clicked the back arrow on the browser and returned to the search results. Halfway down the page, I found what I was looking for: a list of volunteers for the Granville Methodist Church. I clicked the link and scrolled past the description of a fundraiser from two years ago. They were collecting items for a silent auction. At the bottom was Jeff's address as a location to drop off donations.

I cut and pasted the address into my browser. From my apartment, it would take about an hour to get there. I slipped on a pair of shorts and a T-shirt, not stopping to take my usual morning shower. I had to know what was real in Danielle's life.

As I drove towards Danielle's house, I debated what to do when I got there. Could I pretend to be a co-worker who just happened to be in the area? I considered ringing Danielle's doorbell and professing my love. What did I have to lose? I was leaving North Carolina in two months anyway.

After an hour's drive, an expansive housing development came into view. A billboard showed a smiling couple with two kids playing with a dog on a lush green lawn. My GPS told me to make a right into the housing complex. Ironically, I turned onto Durham Way, then made a sharp right onto Chapel Hill Avenue. All the streets were named after North Carolina cities to give the development a sense of cohesiveness. My GPS showed two more right turns until I arrived at Danielle's house. I made a right onto High Point Avenue, where I swerved to avoid two young boys playing basketball in the street.

As I drove closer to Danielle's house, my heart raced. I wiped my palms on my shorts, realizing how moist they had become. The street where Danielle lived dead-ended into a cul-de-sac. I didn't see any movement at her house, but two cars were parked in the driveway, including Danielle's blue minivan. I backed up onto the cross street. The corner house partially blocked my sightline to Danielle's home, but I could see most of her front yard. I closed my eyes and rubbed my temples. What was I doing? Was I stalking Danielle and her family? I was not some serial killer looking for my next victim; I was looking for the woman whom I had fallen in love with.

I realized I should leave before someone called the police to report a suspicious vehicle. As I started my car, several people emerged from Danielle's house. I recognized her husband, Jeff, from his online photo. He threw a baseball with a young boy, whom I assumed was Kyle. Danielle came out of the house with her arm around a teenage girl. The teenager wore a black T-shirt and jeans, her hair dyed a deep purple. She stood about a head taller than Danielle. The two stood on the front steps, talking and laughing. Haley kissed her mother, waved at her stepfather, and backed the minivan out of the driveway.

Was this the horrible life that Danielle was escaping from? This seemed like a typical American family. Was Danielle giving me a load of bullshit so I would sleep with her? Seeing this scene made me feel manipulated, cheap, and angry. Everything she told me about her crappy life was, in fact, crap.

I stared at Danielle's house, twisting my hands on the steering wheel. The vinyl creaked like old leather. I thought I saw Danielle glancing my way. Maybe she could see the front of my LeBaron peeking around the corner. I considered driving down the street and making a U-turn in the cul-de-sac, covertly letting her know I was there.

I decided against that and drove back towards the entrance to the development. Once I could no longer see her house, I stepped on the gas, speeding through the curvy streets. Anger raged through my body. I felt used by Danielle. She wanted to escape from a boring family life, not to have a meaningful relationship with me. Today, she was having a regular Sunday with her husband and family. Less than twenty-four hours ago, we had crazy sex in a field surrounded by lemon trees.

I found myself back at the entrance of the housing complex. Distracted by my thoughts of Danielle, I ran a stop sign and nearly T-boned another car. The driver of a white pickup slammed on his brakes while I skidded across the intersection, barely avoiding a drainage ditch. The pickup truck swerved around me.

"Asshole!"

I took a deep breath and trembled from the adrenaline surge of nearly being hit. I breathed slowly and repeated my mantra, "Danielle is a bitch," over and over.

Finally, I felt calm enough to drive home. Looking twice in each direction, I backed onto the road. I made it home in forty-five minutes. I had little recollection of the ride. I could only remember the rage I felt as I entered my apartment. I flopped down on the bed, not bothering to take off my clothes. Lying on my stomach, I buried my head in my pillow and cried.

"Danielle is a bitch," I repeated until I fell asleep.

38

—·—

MAY 25TH

I was working an overtime shift, doing non-emergent transports to nursing homes and dialysis centers. It was mind-numbing work, and I felt sorry for the EMTs who had to do this job every day. The job was tedious, but I made overtime paramedic money for doing very little work.

We had just loaded Ms. Ethel Thomas into the back of the ambulance. She leaned slightly to her left, staring blankly at the wall. I took her hospital summary from a manila envelope. Ms. Thomas grunted and coughed weakly. I flipped through her paperwork. The eighty-seven-year-old had suffered a massive stroke a week ago. She had bled into her brain, causing paralysis on her right side. She was unable to eat or talk anymore. She received all her nutrition through a feeding tube in her stomach.

I had seen this play out too many times during my short career. Ms. Thomas would be abandoned in a nursing home to spend her remaining few years in bed, her body slowly breaking down. I imagined what this lady's life once was. She looked like a schoolteacher to me. She had five kids and twelve grandchildren. She had been married to her husband for fifty-six years. He had been a war veteran, and they had never been unfaithful during their marriage.

The rest of her years would be spent rotting in bed, a conglomeration of infections invading her body. First would be urinary tract infections, followed by aspiration pneumonias. Eventually, her skin would break down from lying in one position all day. More infections would ravage her body. The doctors would try to clear the infection with antibiotics. Her family, who never visited, would tell the medical staff to "do everything" to keep Ms. Thomas alive, ignoring the patient's suffering and loss of dignity. Ms. Thomas would slowly spiral downwards, each infection bringing her closer to death.

As we bumped along towards the nursing home, I became increasingly depressed. It was a combination of Ms. Thomas' pitiful life and the current state of my relationship with Danielle. A week had passed since I saw the reality of Danielle's house. She had asked to come over on Tuesday, but I had said no for the first time in our relationship. I couldn't figure out how to be with her, knowing that she was lying to me. I thought I was helping her escape from a terrible family situation. After seeing her house and children, I no longer felt like a hero.

My phone chirped and vibrated in my lap. Danielle's message had no words, just a series of question marks. I turned the phone over and put it against my leg. My phone vibrated again. "Are you ignoring me?" I swiped up to dismiss Danielle's message. I couldn't think about her right now.

The ambulance stopped under the front awning of the nursing home. I hastily stuffed Ms. Thomas's discharge papers back into the manila envelope. She would die alone in this nursing home, slowly rotting away. When I thought about Danielle, I felt the same sense of abandonment. I couldn't let her go. The emptiness of my life without Danielle would be overwhelming.

My partner opened the back doors of the ambulance. "We have to find your new room, Ms. Thomas," I announced aloud, doubting any of my words crossed into her brain. With a bounce, we wheeled Mrs. Thompson toward the last room she would ever know.

39

JUNE 2ND

Danielle had called earlier in the day, asking me to meet her at a restaurant halfway between her house and Durham. The college had unexpectedly canceled her nursing classes for the day. She couldn't come to me but wanted to meet me for lunch before her kids came home from school.

I was conflicted as to my next move. I could tell her I didn't want to see her, which might lead to her saying, "fuck it," and not talking to me again, or the act of saying no could make her want me more. On the other hand, I could say yes and reiterate what I genuinely wanted: for her to move to New Orleans with me. That path could permanently end our relationship, or I could finally get the answer I wanted.

I agreed to meet Danielle for lunch at The End of the Road restaurant. When I arrived, Danielle's minivan was already parked in the lot. I climbed into the passenger side of her van. No words were exchanged before we kissed, our mouths exploring each other. We kissed until we heard some giggling from the car next to us. Two young girls were pointing and making faces. We laughed with embarrassment and waved back at the two kids.

The End of the Road was a casual restaurant that catered to families and those looking for a simple meal. The room was ringed with vinyl-covered booths and a faded red carpet with worn areas where the floor was visible. All the décor was cheap, down to the paper placemats with advertisements for local businesses. I motioned to an empty table in the middle of the room, but Danielle walked to a booth in the corner, partially obscured by a wall. We sat and looked at our menus. Mine was sticky from the fingers of the last guest.

"How was your day?" It was a lame question, but as this was our first time out together in public, I tried to make normal relationship conversation.

"Jeff took the kids to his mother's, so I slept in. It was a pleasant change from my usual day. What about you?"

"I thought a lot about you." I reached across the table and touched her hand. Danielle frowned. She seemed to have no interest in physical contact. The waitress came, and we both ordered our meals.

"For real, what did you do today?"

"I hung around the apartment watching TV." If I weren't interacting with Danielle, I wouldn't be interacting with anyone. She had become the singular focus of my life. She was meant to go to New Orleans with me. She was the person I was meant to grow old with. I was angry that she did not share my vision of our future. I took a deep breath to focus on the present. "It's nice to be out with you, someplace other than my bedroom."

As we waited for our food, Danielle continuously glanced around the restaurant. She tapped her fingers nervously on the table. Her shoulders were hunched, and she seemed on edge. Suddenly, she leaned over and covered her face with her hand.

"What's wrong?" From how she hid, I thought her husband had walked in. I looked to our right and saw two women sitting down at a booth diagonally across from us. Danielle's eyes darted left and right. "What's going on?"

The waitress brought our meals, but Danielle immediately pushed her plate away. "This was a huge mistake, Adam." Without a word, she got up and put on her jacket.

I grabbed her arm and pulled her back into the booth. "What are you talking about?"

"One of the women sitting at the next table has a daughter in Haley's class. She's the biggest gossip in the school. If she sees us, it'll be all over fucking town. Everybody will know about us. What a fucking mistake this was!"

I held Danielle's arm tightly so she couldn't get off the bench. "Her back is to us. We're fine."

"Adam, let go of me. I need to get out of here." She yanked her arm away. "Don't follow me."

She walked to the exit with her head down. I didn't understand why she was embarrassed to be seen with me. I was younger, smarter, and more successful than her husband. If we were going to have a life together, we couldn't just meet for sex a few times a week. We needed to have a real relationship.

Without waiting for a check, I left a twenty-dollar bill on the table and walked out of the restaurant. It had only been a few minutes since Danielle left, but her car was already gone. A horn honked at me from behind. I'd been standing in the middle of the parking lot, lost in thought. I waved apologetically.

As I drove home on the Durham Freeway, I was shaking. This afternoon was to be our first real date, but it ended with her running away from me. I slammed my fist against the steering wheel, causing the car to cross into the next lane.

"Fuck!" I yelled at the top of my lungs and then started crying. I wiped my eyes with the back of my hand, realizing I was losing Danielle. Perhaps 'losing' was the wrong word since I never truly had her.

As I drove down the Durham Freeway, I crossed under bridges supported by large, round, concrete pylons. I unclipped my seatbelt. My LeBaron had no airbags. If I drove full speed into one of the concrete pillars, it would be chalked up to an accident, another careless young man speeding down the highway. I wondered if anyone would care that I was dead.

I gripped the steering wheel with two hands. If I moved to the right just a little, I could hit one of those pylons straight on. It was so tempting. A future without Danielle seemed like no future at all. I took a deep breath and kept the car pointed straight down the highway. Fuck her. I would not let Danielle dominate my thoughts and actions. I would control the ending of my story.

40

— · —

June 18th

I sat in the passenger seat of the ambulance, thinking about Danielle. I was so distracted that I could barely function at work. I thought about her day and night. I could see her lying on the pillow next to me when I fell asleep. I could taste her on my lips when I woke up.

My driving privileges at work had been suspended as I had been in two ambulance accidents in a week. Last week, I had sideswiped a car as I pulled away from a curb, causing considerable damage to the small sedan. Two days ago, I beached the ambulance in the median of a highway. We had been responding to a respiratory distress call. We were driving down a four-lane road divided by a grassy median that sloped downwards in the center. I had missed the crossover in the median, and it was a mile until the next turnaround. I figured if I gunned the ambulance across the median, I could make it to the other side. Without asking my partner, I turned the wheel to the left and accelerated into the median. Between the weight of the ambulance, the mud from the previous night's rain, and the incline to the street, I wedged the truck in the grass. Not only did we have to call another ambulance to respond, but I also caused over $20,000 in damage to the ambulance. I was unsure of the final disciplinary action, but for the near future, I would only be allowed to ride in the passenger seat or in the back with patients.

My phone vibrated with a text alert. "Are we still meeting at the park tonight?" This would be our first time together since our lunch had been interrupted.

She replied with a heart and a sexy wink emoji.

In the last two weeks, I mainly felt anger towards Danielle. I felt lied to and dirty. Everything she had told me about her husband and marriage was false. She might have some marital problems, but after seeing her at her house, her life didn't seem as bad as she described.

Now, it was my turn to use Danielle for sex. I no longer wanted her in my life after I left North Carolina. I was going to release my emotional attachment to her. Our relationship would be strictly physical for the next month and nothing more. If she could use me for sex, I could use her.

Jennifer asked me if I felt okay as I remained quiet throughout our ride back to base. I leaned my head against the window with my eyes closed. It was 6:45 P.M.; if all went well, we would be off on time.

"Adam? Hello?"

"Sorry, I was just a little distracted thinking about my move to New Orleans."

"Really? Is that why you were distracted?"

"The whole driving thing is a mess. I know I only have a month left here, but I don't want to leave looking like a douche who can't drive."

"I heard your date with Danielle did not end well." I didn't respond. "Adam, don't worry about it. You'll be out of here in a month and never look back. You will never see her again. No one will care about your driving." We stopped at a red light. She squeezed my hand, and I looked over at her. "Partner, I've thoroughly enjoyed working with you over the past few months. You will be an incredible doctor."

"Thanks, Jen. I've enjoyed working with you too."

Jennifer backed the ambulance into the bay. We both opened our doors, but I grabbed her hand. "Jennifer, you've saved my ass several times. I couldn't have done it without you as my partner."

"As much as I love Danielle, tell her to go fuck herself."

41

— • —

JUNE 18TH

Although I finished my shift on time, Danielle texted that she was on a late call, and it would be at least an hour until she left work. We planned to meet at Rock Ridge Park for a brief rendezvous. She wouldn't be there until close to 8:30 P.M., and I had to work the following day, but the excitement of sex with Danielle in a public place was too much temptation.

"Let me know when you leave," I texted, and she replied with a thumbs up.

I no longer felt the same passion for Danielle that I had two weeks ago. I now felt negative emotions when I thought of her: sadness and anger. At this point, sex was for pure satisfaction, nothing more.

I stopped at a convenience store to kill time, filling my car with half a tank of gas and grabbing a bottle of iced tea. I was annoyed at having to wait for Danielle. Being late was not her fault, but I had lost the sense of complete forgiveness I had for her. I would no longer be her toy, bending to her whims.

At 8:00 P.M., Danielle texted me that she was leaving work. She would be at the park by 8:30 P.M. I tapped my fingers on the steering wheel. Patience never came easily to me, and I hated wasting time.

I didn't move the car until Danielle texted that she had arrived at the park. Although I was only ten minutes away, she would have to wait for me. Daylight faded as I spotted a dark brown sign with white paint marking the entrance to Rock Ridge Park. A single paved road ringed an artificial lake. Along the water's edge were benches, playgrounds, and picnic tables.

I drove slowly as there was no ambient light in the park. Suddenly, my headlights were reflected by two yellow circles in the middle of the road. I slammed on the brakes. A raccoon stared at me as if to ask why I was driving on its road. Finally, it picked up a piece of trash and scampered into the bushes.

I drove along the one-lane road until I saw a pair of brake lights in the back of the most distant lot. I parked next to Danielle's minivan and climbed into the front seat. Without a word, Danielle pulled me towards her, and we kissed. I was aroused, but this kiss felt different. I was more excited about the possibility of being caught than by being with Danielle herself.

Danielle must have sensed something was off because she looked at me quizzically. "Is anything wrong?"

I didn't respond and went back to kissing her. We made out, her hands exploring under my shirt. I reciprocated and played with her breasts. I felt her nipples become erect. She reached down between my legs and stroked me. We kissed more deeply, making love with our tongues. Finally, she started unbuttoning my uniform pants. She leaned over and took me in her mouth, bobbing up and down. I sat back with my hands clasped behind my head, enjoying the pleasure. After a few minutes, she leaned her seat back, pulling me on top of her. I hovered over her, my pants around my ankles. I looked out the back window of the minivan and saw only darkness.

"You feel so fucking good, Adam." I was aroused by how excited I made her. I enjoyed having this married woman under me. She wanted to sleep with me, not her husband. I thrusted at my tempo, not hers. I was the one who satisfied her.

She encouraged me. "Faster, Adam, faster!" I pumped in and out of her. At this point, I was not feeling pleasure. I was feeling rage. I harnessed that anger to move faster and deeper. Danielle didn't notice. Her eyes were shut. Her fingernails dug into my lower back. I became more frenzied, and she became louder. I sped up and watched her face. She turned her head from right to left, yelling, "Just like that! Just like that!"

I watched Danielle squirm with pleasure. In an angry voice, I said, "You like that, don't you?" Danielle nodded. "Say you like it," I commanded.

"I like it, Adam. I fucking love it." Danielle moaned submissively.

"You like it when I fuck you, don't you?" I hissed at her. She nodded again. "Tell me you fucking like it!"

"Fuck me more, Adam!"

Danielle pulled me deep inside her. The explicit talk was turning me on more than the sex itself. I felt powerful. I was intoxicated by my ability to excite her.

"Do you like it when your young stud fucks you?"

Immediately after I spoke those words, I knew I had taken a wrecking ball to our relationship. Danielle stopped moving, and her head snapped forward. She looked me straight in the eyes, a mix of disgust and shame. She pushed herself off of me, accidentally beeping the horn. Danielle scrambled to get her pants off the floorboard. She opened the door, not caring that she was naked from the waist down.

"Why would you say something like that, you fucking asshole? Get the fuck out of my car!"

I stumbled out of the car, pulling up my pants awkwardly. Danielle ignored me as she got dressed. She got back into her car and glared at me with anger.

"Adam, you are a piece of shit. I never want to hear from you again. I never want to see you again."

I fumbled to button my pants. I kept the passenger door open, hoping she would calm down and tell me what had happened.

"Danielle, just take a deep breath."

Danielle looked at me with complete hatred. With an icy voice, she said, "Don't you ever fucking call me again." She shifted into reverse with the passenger door still open. I barely had time to jump out of the way as gravel sprayed from the tires. The van fishtailed slightly as she slammed on the brakes. She shifted into drive while still moving backward, grinding the gears. As she accelerated forward, the door slammed closed. With the screeching of tires, I watched the minivan's brake lights fly around a curve and out of sight.

I looked through the darkness and saw a glimmer of moonlight reflect off the pond. A crescent moon shone through the trees. I closed my eyes and felt my body become void of energy. My last real connection with anyone in North Carolina had been severed.

The analytical part of my brain knew that what I said was unfixable. My mouth had once again gotten me in trouble. Although I was angry with Danielle, I didn't want to hurt her.

I loved her. Despite what had happened tonight, part of me still believed we could be together. I leaned against the trunk of my car, thinking, dreaming, and imagining an alternative future without Danielle. A fog floated across the black sky, mirroring the cloudiness of my thoughts.

I drove home slowly, my jaw tight, angry at myself for hurting Danielle. I loved her; that would never change. I didn't want this night to be the way we ended our relationship. I wanted her to remember me as the man who brought pleasure back into her life. I needed one more chance to make her happy.

42

JULY 14TH

I drove through the employee entrance of the parking garage across from Duke Hospital. I made a quick right-hand turn and took a short ramp down to the bottom level. Piedmont EMS had recently opened its new Duke base on the bottom floor of the structure.

I hadn't spoken to Danielle for nearly a month, but I thought about her every day. I felt guilty that my words had cut her so deeply. Between the move to New Orleans and my obsession with Danielle, I tossed and turned in bed every night, my mind racing.

A bouquet of a dozen yellow roses lay on the seat next to me. The florist had told me that yellow was the color for apologies. I knew I had screwed up in the park. I couldn't get Danielle on the phone. I couldn't get her to respond to my text messages. It was so twisted. I still wanted her to move to New Orleans with me.

I invented a story to explain why I was at the base on my day off: I had left my earbuds in the bunk room. I didn't even own earbuds, but I figured it would make a plausible story. I tapped my ID badge against the card reader, and the lock clicked open.

To my surprise, Jennifer was napping on the couch. I heard her take a little snore and gasp for air, and then her eyes opened. "What are you doing here on a Sunday?"

"I forgot my earbuds here last week."

"Bullshit, partner. I assume you're here to see Danielle." I nodded. "She's in the bunk room taking a nap."

The bunkroom was dark and cool, a wonderful place to sleep. There were no windows, and on Sunday, there was little ambient noise from cars. Gray metal frames supported two single beds on either side of the room. Danielle lay motionless under a white hospital blanket. I had come to know the outline of her body. I knew the way her hair fell when she slept. I wanted to crawl into bed and curl around her. She would feel our bodies together and realize she wanted to spend the rest of her life with me.

"Are you awake?" I whispered as I stood in the doorway. Danielle turned over on her back. She squinted at me through the fluorescent light streaming through the door.

"What the fuck are you doing here?"

"You haven't returned any of my calls or texts, so I thought I'd stop by to check in and see how you're doing."

"I don't want to talk to you. I made it clear that we're done." Jennifer was on the couch, leafing through a magazine, though I knew she was straining to hear us.

I sat on the bed at Danielle's feet. "Look, Danielle, I'm truly sorry for what I said that night. I didn't realize my words would be so hurtful to you. We were in the middle of sex, and they just came out." I stuttered, trying to say the words. "I wish I could take them back. I want us back to how we were, even for another month."

Danielle slipped her feet into her boots without lacing them. "Let's walk outside. I don't need Jennifer telling the world my business."

We walked through the crew room and into the parking lot. I reached out and took Danielle's hand, but she pulled it back. "I have something for you." I took the yellow roses out of my car and offered them to her. "I know I can't take the words back. How can I make this right?"

I expected Danielle to smile, for the flowers to melt her heart, and for her to realize what a romantic guy I was. She pushed them back towards me.

"You just don't get it. We had a lot of fun, but that's all it was. I cannot say this any more clearly: we are not together. We will not talk on the phone or text. We will not see each other. I know you fantasized about a future for us together. It is a future that cannot not exist." She touched my chin with her index finger. "I have children and a husband, and I won't leave them."

My shoulders slumped noticeably, and the energy drained from my body. Danielle reached up with her right hand and cupped my face. She looked directly into my eyes, no longer with anger but with pity. "Adam, I want you to listen, because I will only say this once. You are an amazing, handsome, intelligent guy, and I know you'll be a successful doctor. One day, you will find a woman who will be your perfect mate, but I am not her."

Danielle kissed me on the cheek. It was perfunctory, but then she made a surprising move. She stood on her tiptoes and kissed on the lips. me. Her lips lingered on mine. I closed my eyes, enjoying what would likely be the last time I would feel her touch. She pulled her mouth away but kept her hand on my cheek.

"Go live your life." She walked into the EMS office, never looking back.

I stood in the parking lot with my hands at my side; the roses pointed down at the cement. A car drove slowly past, and the elderly driver stared at me. I put the roses on the hood of Danielle's minivan. There was no longer anything for me in North Carolina. I could see Danielle and Jennifer talking through the glass pane in the door. Were they talking about me?

Distracted, I almost hit a parked car as I backed out of my parking spot. I had lost Allison and Danielle. The Bull City had nothing left for me. Fuck Durham! My life could only get better in New Orleans.

43

AUGUST 2ND

I had just finished my last shift as a paramedic at Piedmont EMS. I had two weeks before I moved to New Orleans. My last EMS call was a seventy-eight-year-old woman who had slipped on the floor and injured her left ankle. This call certainly did not require paramedic-level care. I could have left it to my EMT partner, but as it was my last call before I headed to medical school, I wanted to take one more opportunity to ride in the back of an ambulance. I worked on the patient care report as we returned to the station. This would be the last time I signed my name to an EMS chart. I handed off my radio to the oncoming medic and completed my last transfer of the controlled substance box.

I looked around the main EMS base at the tattered furniture, well-worn carpets, and stained ceiling tiles. I didn't think I would be emotional on my last shift, but I was sad as I left the station. My work as a paramedic had earned me a spot in medical school. No one except Jennifer and Wayne knew that today was my last day. I didn't want to make a big deal of it because people would start bringing food and cakes. I wanted to walk off quietly into the sunset.

Wayne shouted to me as I walked to my car, "Are you going to Sirens tomorrow?" A few of the employees from our platoon were celebrating their promotions. I had been to Sirens once, but strip clubs were never my thing. I found it exciting for a few minutes, but by the time I left, I felt like I needed decontamination. The stench of bad perfume mixed with stale cigarettes was nauseating. Not to mention, I went home with hundreds of dollars less than when I walked into the club.

Since I never planned on returning to Durham, I figured, what the hell? "Wayne, I will see you tomorrow!"

44

AUGUST 3RD

I woke up on Tuesday morning with plans to pack my apartment for my move to New Orleans. It was a beautiful summer day, ninety degrees, with a clear blue sky. I took a walk around the apartment complex just to be outside. I watched a baseball game on television, killing time until 8:00 P.M.

Sirens was twenty minutes away in Raleigh. Its neon lights glowed brightly over the highway, advertising live dancers, nudity, and cold beer. The rest of the area was dark, filled with warehouses and office complexes, void of activity at night.

As I walked to the front door, I passed a group of men standing outside the club smoking cigarettes and bad weed. They talked excitedly about the dancers in the club. I heard snippets of their conversation.

"Did you see when she stuck her tits in my face?"

"What an ass that chick had!"

"I'd like to take her home for a hundred bucks."

As I passed, one of the men blew a cloud of smoke my way. "Want a hit?" I ignored him. I thought about turning around and leaving. I was already disgusted by the smoke, the other patrons, and the music blasting out of the club. I figured I would make an appearance, have a drink, and leave.

I walked through the front door, where a skinny man in a cheap suit checked my ID. Next to him stood a large bald man providing security. He was about six feet tall and stood as wide as the door. I smiled at him, and he sneered back. The skinny man stamped my hand and grunted I could enter.

Streams of light pulsed around me. Some beams flashed from the ceiling while lasers shot up from the stage. A topless woman wrapped herself around a pole. She bent herself backward in half and seemed to smile directly at me. She jiggled her breasts, and they barely moved. They were way too round for a woman who appeared to be in her early forties. The room was fairly empty, so it was easy to spot my coworkers on the far side of the room. As I walked around the stage, the stripper's eyes followed me like one of those creepy paintings in a haunted house.

I saw five of my EMS coworkers sitting around a long table facing the stage: Wayne, Jennifer, Mike, and Erica, the latter two of whom were celebrating their graduation from paramedic school. Sitting next to Mike was Danielle, a person I never thought I would see again. As I approached the table, she paid no attention to me. She did not even make eye contact. She pressed her body against Mike's, rubbing his goatee. Everyone at the table had a bottle of beer in front of them. With the empties in front of her, Danielle had already drank three or four of them. I watched Mike put his arm around Danielle, pulling her tighter against him.

I sat down next to Wayne at the opposite end of the table, but I couldn't take my eyes off Danielle. Anger rose inside me as she touched Mike again on the face. I stared at them, transfixed. Was she touching Mike on purpose to skewer me, or was she really such a whore that she would get with that fat fuck?

Mike, an EMT who had worked for Piedmont EMS for eight years, had finally passed his paramedic certification on the third attempt. Although Mike was six feet three inches, most of his weight centered around his midsection. He always looked disheveled, with his uniform shirt untucked from his pants and often open in the front. His goatee extruded messily from his chin.

"Sweetie, do you want anything?" a server asked me, dangling her breasts in my face. Her tight white T-shirt did little to hide her cleavage. I was so distracted by Danielle that the waitress had to ask me again.

Wayne slapped me on the shoulder. "Let me buy you a beer. Bring us both a Miller Lite," Wayne told the waitress.

"Sure thing, sweetie." I watched her stride away in tight spandex shorts. I turned my attention back to the other end of the table. Mike and Danielle pressed themselves together. I stared at them, but neither seemed to notice. Mike touched Danielle's nose, and she laughed. Was she fucking with me?

Wayne slapped me on the shoulder again and motioned to the stage. "What do you think of her?"

A young woman, who looked to be twenty, had just taken the stage. Music was blaring as she paraded around in a Catholic school uniform, a tiny plaid skirt barely covering her ass. The last two buttons of the shirt were open, revealing a perfectly oblong belly button. She bent over and grabbed her legs. Her skirt rode up, showing the audience everything underneath. There were whistles and claps. She strutted around the stage, slowly unbuttoning her shirt.

A redheaded woman approached the table. She wore tight jean shorts and a halter top that accentuated her large breasts.

"Who here wants a lap dance?"

"How much?" Mike pulled a wad of twenties out of his pocket. The redhead draped her arm gently over Mike's shoulder. It was amazing how these women could reach into men's pockets and suck out the money like a vacuum cleaner. "For you, honey, I would do sixty."

"It's not for me," Mike said with a laugh. "It's for her." He pointed at Danielle with the beer bottle in his hand.

"For this cutie, I would do forty." The dancer kissed Danielle on the cheek.

"Get the fuck out of here." Danielle laughed, but she blushed at the same time.

Mike peeled off two twenties from his bankroll and stuffed the bills right between the stripper's breasts. Danielle bowed her head in acquiescence. The stripper turned Danielle's chair around so her legs were no longer under the table. She straddled Danielle's lap and started grinding against her.

I had to admit that this was one of the hottest things I had ever seen. All three men and Erica, who favored women, had their eyes glued to this lap dance. Only Jennifer leaned back in her chair and shook her head. This was the girl-on-girl action that every man fantasized about.

The redhead reached behind her neck and untied her halter top, leaving her bare-chested. She ran the fabric gently across Danielle's face. She ground rhythmically on Danielle's lap. Finally, she took Danielle's head and buried it between her breasts.

"Oh, shit," Mike said, sounding like he was about to explode. We all agreed with that sentiment.

After the song ended, the dancer fastened her halter top. The experience might have lasted two minutes, but it felt like we had watched for an hour. The dancer kissed Danielle softly on the lips.

"I'll dance for you any time," she said to Danielle as she walked away, blowing a kiss over her shoulder.

Danielle swigged a beer as Mike, Wayne, Erica, and Jennifer hooted. I sat motionless, anger boiling up inside my chest. Was Danielle behaving this way because I was there?

Mike whispered in Danielle's ear. "Ready to get out of here?"

"Let me use the bathroom first."

I watched this exchange with an unbelievable sense of rage. What was Danielle doing? Was she going home with Mike?

Danielle stumbled towards the back of the club, a neon sign pointing the way to the women's room. As she walked, she held onto the wall.

"I am not letting this happen," I mumbled to myself. I followed Danielle towards the bathroom. She had already gone inside, so I leaned against the wall opposite the door. A bulletin board advertised upcoming events: a famous porn star would be dancing next Wednesday and there was a free lunch buffet every Monday afternoon.

Danielle came out of the bathroom and didn't say a word to me as she walked past. It was like she had forgotten everything that had happened between us. I grabbed her arm. She looked at me blankly but didn't pull away.

"Are you really leaving with Mike?" Her mouth tried to form words, but nothing came out.

"Why do you care?" The way she asked the question was strange. She did not seem angry but confused. Why *did* I care who she slept with? She had told me a month ago that she wanted nothing more to do with me. I was moving in two weeks. I would never see Danielle again. She had fucked me, then fucked with my feelings.

I should have turned around and walked out the door, but I didn't move. "I'm not letting you leave with Mike."

Why was I still involved in Danielle's life? I hated Danielle, but at the same time, I loved her like no woman before. I had confused sex with love, that was for sure, but I refused to let Mike take advantage of her. "I'm getting you out of here." She nodded passively and leaned against me.

With my arm around Danielle, I led her around the stage, opposite where our colleagues were sitting. I hurried towards the door so they would not see us, but Danielle was staggering and putting her entire weight on me.

I heard Mike holler from across the stage, "Where are you going, Danielle? Get back here." I'm sure he thought he was getting lucky tonight. I pulled Danielle towards the front door. Mike walked towards us quickly, but his foot caught on a table leg, and he fell to the ground, landing on his hands and knees. I pulled Danielle faster towards the exit.

My car was parked only a few steps away. My LeBaron did not have electric locks, so I propped Danielle against the car, supporting her with one arm while I unlocked the door with the other. I pushed her inside, and she slumped into the front seat. I looked back and didn't see Mike. He outweighed me by over one hundred pounds and was six inches taller than I was. There was no way I could beat him in a physical altercation.

I turned on the engine and opened the windows as Danielle and I both reeked of smoke. Danielle was leaning against the door frame, her brown hair flaring wildly. I didn't realize how short her dress was. She had kicked off her sandals, and I could see her toenails painted a deep shade of red. I had forgotten how attracted I was to her.

I gently touched her cheek with the back of my hand. The feel of her skin brought back memories of lying beside her in bed. I looked down her dress to see her black, lacy bra, which fastened in the front. I loved to unsnap that bra and play with her breasts. I remembered the feeling of her on top of me as we made love. I brushed her thigh with my hand, remembering what it felt like with those smooth legs wrapped around me.

I pulled my hand back. She had no comprehension of my presence. She quietly snored with each breath. It was now 10:30 P.M. What was I going to do? I had a passed-out drunk woman in the front seat of my car. I couldn't exactly drop her off at her house. I thought about driving her back to my apartment, but how could I get her inside? At this point, I didn't think Danielle could navigate a flight of steps to the second floor. I could leave her in the car at my apartment complex overnight, but I'm sure someone would call the police.

I drove down the service road next to the interstate. Danielle was still snoring gently in the passenger seat. I noticed a motel with a neon sign flashing "vacancy." That would be the easiest place for us to stay the night. Danielle retched twice as I prayed she didn't throw up in my car.

I pulled under the motel's awning and looked into the front lobby. A clerk sat behind the reception desk, looking at his phone. He appeared uninterested as I stepped into the lobby.

"Do you have any rooms available?"

He punched a few keys on an old computer. "It looks like we have one room on the third floor. A king bed, if that's good for the two of you," motioning to the car.

"Is there an elevator on the outside?"

"The elevator is through the lobby behind me." How could I get Danielle into the hotel room? At this point, I wasn't even sure she could walk. She was becoming increasingly difficult to arouse since we left the club. I couldn't be seen carrying a half-drunk woman through the lobby.

"Nothing on the first floor?"

"Only a single."

"I'll take it."

"Sixty-six dollars." I paused as I pulled out my credit card. Was I going to pay for this debacle? I considered taking a credit card from Danielle's wallet, but realized her husband might see the charge. Why did I care about Daniele's marriage anyway? I handed my credit card across the desk, and the clerk handed me back an old-fashioned key with a tag marked Room 118. "Make two rights and you'll see the room."

I mumbled, "Thank you," as I left the lobby. I found a parking spot directly in front of the room. Through the large picture window, I saw a single dingy bed and an oversized chair. I unlocked the room and propped the door open with a garbage can. The room had a strong marijuana smell. The last occupants had ignored the no smoking signs.

I opened the passenger door and grabbed Danielle by the shoulders as she fell out. I groaned as I caught her weight.

"Let's get you inside."

Danielle looked up at me, and for a moment, our eyes locked. I felt that connection we once had. She reached up towards my face as if to touch it, but instead said, "I feel like I'm going to throw up."

She put her arm around my shoulder, and I put mine around her waist, pulling her into the musty hotel room. Danielle retched again, and I steered her towards the bathroom. She kneeled in front of the toilet, dry heaving.

I looked at the grime on the shower wall and the black mold growing on the grout. The shower curtain was stained brown with mystery fluids, and the fixtures in the bathroom looked like they hadn't been replaced in forty years.

"It's so fucking hot in here!" Danielle pulled her black dress over her head, leaving her in only her bra and underwear.

I sat on the side of the bathtub and clasped my hands, trying to grasp my current situation. I was in a dingy motel room with a married woman with whom I had a six-month affair. She was past drunk, dry heaving over a filthy toilet in a disgusting bathroom. I stroked her head, running my fingers through her long brown hair. I took a strand and ran it under my nose. The scent of her strawberry shampoo brought back memories of her lying on my chest.

"Water," Danielle croaked.

Two glasses were sitting on the sink, covered with a paper wrapper. I wondered if they had ever been washed. I filled one glass halfway and handed it to Danielle. Keeping her eyes closed, she took a small sip.

"I'm so dizzy," she whined. I grabbed the glass from her hand as her grip loosened, spilling water on the floor. She looked up at me.

"Call Jeff," she whined. I ignored her. Her head bobbed as she tried to stay awake. "Call Jeff! Call my fucking husband!"

Anger boiled inside me. Was she really asking me to call her husband? Danielle lay on the bathroom floor, curled in the fetal position. Then she started crying. She pounded her fists on the tile floor like a three-year-old.

"Call my husband!" she yelled repeatedly. I was sure that the occupants of the next room would call the front desk to complain or, even worse, call the police.

"Fuck you," I muttered as I stood up. I was cursing both Danielle and me. Why was I in a motel room taking care of this woman who had betrayed me?

"Call your own fucking husband!" I slammed the glass on the sink, surprised it didn't shatter in my hand.

I walked to the front window. In the parking lot, two young men stood around a beat-up Oldsmobile smoking a joint. A motorcycle revved its engine. I could see the headlights of the cars on the interstate passing at high speeds. I stood at the window, debating whether to walk out the door. Danielle was just drunk. She would wake up in the morning and be fine.

I stepped from the air-conditioned room into the humid North Carolina summer night. Through the window, I could see Danielle still lying in the bathroom. What if she choked on her vomit and died in a motel room that I had rented with my credit card? As betrayed and angry as I was, I could not leave Danielle on that filthy bathroom floor. I still felt responsible for her. I also feared I would go to jail if something happened to her.

I re-entered the room and closed the curtain across the large window. When I flipped the light switch, a single bulb flickered overhead, attracting flying insects.

I squatted down next to Danielle who was still lying on the bathroom floor. She was taking slow, deep breaths. Her lips fluttered with each exhalation. She was now naked except for her black lace thong; her bra lay next to her. I stared at her body. Less than a month ago, I was infatuated with Danielle. The body lying in front of me was the object of my dreams every night.

I shook her gently on the shoulder. "Danielle, let's get into bed. This floor's filthy."

I put my arms under her shoulders and propped her against my knee. "Get off me!" she said, her words slurring. Her head flopped down into her chest.

"Up we go." I lifted her from under her arms.

"Get off of me, Mike!" She flung her arms backward. Did she think I was Mike?

"Get the fuck up!" She tried to push me away, but the force caused her to stumble backward onto the bed.

"It's not Mike," I said disgustedly. "It's Adam. I'm the one who fucking loves you!" She looked at me and opened her eyes wide. For a second, I thought I saw the same glimmer in her eyes as I did on Halloween, but then she started snoring.

She had fallen asleep with her legs hanging over the side of the bed. I pulled the blanket back and swung her legs on top. I covered her with the sheet, leaving only her head exposed. I watched her sleep. I ran my hand over her face. I kissed her lightly on the lips.

She opened her eyes, and she smiled at me. I became aroused. I kissed her again, but as soon as I touched her lips, she swatted me away like a mosquito.

"Can you please call my fucking husband?" Danielle started crying again. My arousal quickly dissipated.

"Are you crazy? You want *me* to call *your* husband?"

Increasingly, she sounded like a scared child crying out for a parent. Life did not have to turn out this way for Danielle. I would have cared for her, supported her, and given her stability. She rolled around on the bed. "Call my husband!"

"Danielle, stop it!" I grabbed her shoulders and held her on her back. I looked into her eyes. "Danielle, it's Adam. I'll take care of you." I pleaded with her to calm down. I rubbed her head. "Danielle, I'm not calling your fucking husband!" Finally, I gave up and sat in the chair facing the window. I covered my ears to drown out Danielle's screaming.

A man in the next room slammed his fist against the wall. "Would you all shut the fuck up?"

I was caught between two bad choices. I could leave, but I was still afraid something terrible could happen to Danielle before she sobered up. The other choice was to call her husband. Each time she yelled for her husband, I felt a stab in my chest. I needed her to shut up. I had no idea where her cell phone was. She didn't have a purse or a bag with her.

"Danielle," I said resignedly, "what's Jeff's number?"

The motel still had an old-fashioned push-button phone, the kind with the little red light to alert the occupants that the front desk was holding a message. The buttons were once white but had faded into a tan color. I picked up the receiver and prepared to dial the number. Danielle quickly rattled off numbers that made no sense at all.

"Slow down!" I snapped. My head was pounding from her yelling, and my eyes were irritated by the leftover smoke in the room.

Finally, Danielle gave me a coherent phone number. I cringed as I dialed, feeling shame, anger, and guilt. The phone rang, and I handed it over to Danielle. She reached for the headset but lacked the coordination to hold it herself. I held the phone to her ear. A male voice answered, sounding sleepy.

"Come pick me up," Danielle mumbled into the phone. "Pick me up now!" I walked over to the window, not wanting to hear this conversation.

The phone dropped from Danielle's head onto the bed, and I could hear the man's distant voice. "How can I pick you up if I don't know where the fuck you are?"

Danielle yelled at me in a slurred voice. "Tell him where I'm at!" She reached awkwardly around her head to find the phone but kept missing the headset. I picked up the receiver and stared at it in my hand. Was I going to talk to her husband, the man with whose wife I had been sleeping with for months?

"Hello?" I heard Jeff ask. I put the phone to my mouth, but I couldn't get words out. "Hello?" Jeff asked again.

I finally croaked out some words. "She's at the Raleigh Motel off the Interstate, room 118."

"I'll be there when I get off work at six." There was a click, followed by silence and a dial tone. I left the phone off the hook so he could not call back.

By this time, Danielle had fallen asleep under the sheets. I pulled the cover back. She was naked from the waist up. The basest part of me thought about waking her up just to have sex with her. She owed me. I saved her from spending the night with Mike. I paid for this room and made sure she was safe.

I gently rolled her onto her back. I remembered how much I loved to play with her nipples as we made love. I ran the back of my hand over her belly. I traced the scars on her lower abdomen. Staying on top of her underwear, I touched between her legs and could feel her heat. By this time, I was so aroused. I wanted so much to pull down her thong and have sex one last time with her, but that wasn't me. I couldn't have sex with a barely conscious woman, no matter how much lust I felt.

I moved to the oversized chair in the corner of the room., waiting for my arousal to subside. I slipped off my shoes and propped my feet on the edge of the bed. The clock on the nightstand read 2:45 A.M. I closed my eyes and let my head fall back. What was I doing with my life? I needed to get to New Orleans.

I fell asleep briefly but woke up around 4:30 A.M. to use the bathroom. As I unwrapped the cheap bar of soap, I looked at myself in the mirror. Was I a good person or a bad one? Was I the hero or the idiot?

I sat back in the chair and had vivid dreams over the next hour and a half. I dreamed of Danielle and me lying together on a beach while our children played in the sun and surf. Were they her kids or our kids? I dreamed Allison had slapped me across the face. I felt the sting on my cheek, and my nose started to bleed.

Three loud thumps woke me from sleep. I pulled back the curtain to see a man knocking at the door. He wore a white uniform shirt and blue pants, a North Carolina paramedic patch on his sleeve. He pounded on the door three times again. I wiped away the spit that had gathered on the side of my mouth. I grabbed my car keys from the table next to the bed. I was getting out of that room as fast as I could.

When I opened the door, Danielle's husband had a snarl on his face. He did not like finding his drunk wife in a cheap motel with another man. I didn't explain what happened. I looked him square in the eye and pointed at Danielle, still sleeping on the bed.

"She's your problem now." I squeezed past Jeff and climbed into my car. I quickly backed out of the parking space, my tires squealing. It was time for a new life.

45

— · —

SEPTEMBER 3RD, TWO YEARS LATER

A hurricane was coming to New Orleans. It was only Tuesday, and the storm was not scheduled to hit the city until Friday. All the schools and universities had already closed, allowing their students to evacuate. New Orleans had shut down its tourist attractions to encourage visitors to leave.

I lived in a one-bedroom apartment in the Warehouse District, about ten blocks from the French Quarter. With the city ready to be attacked by a hurricane in three days, the sky pretended that perfect weather was ahead. Except for the barrage of announcements about the hurricane, it seemed like a typical day in New Orleans. Taxis drove past. I could hear the bell of the streetcar. In a few hours, the interstate would be made one-directional, allowing traffic to flow only out of the city. I would go to Baton Rouge to find a hotel until New Orleans was declared safe.

My transition from working as a paramedic in Durham to medical school was the most challenging experience of my life. I moved to a new city where I knew no one, started challenging classes, and felt isolated from my peers. I considered pursuing another romantic relationship, as I hated the loneliness of my life. I still hadn't resolved my feelings for Allison and Danielle, and those thoughts held me back from forming a connection with another woman.

My rage at Allison haunted me at night, even though we hadn't spoken in over three years. I thought of her frequently, imagining our marriage that should've been and our life that never was. After that Valentine's Day, Allison and I hadn't spoken on the phone. I texted her a couple of times, wanting to apologize for that night. I knew we did not have a future together, but I still loved her. My text messages went unanswered. In the Duke newsletter, I read that she had won several awards as a medical student. Every so often, I would check her social media or search for her name online. I never found out if she was dating someone else, but with each search, I saw a new academic publication or accolade.

My relationship with Danielle also weighed on me. I texted her the night after the hotel, wanting to say goodbye, but she had blocked my number. On my phone, I only had one photo of us together. It was from an afternoon we had spent together in my apartment. She looked so peaceful as we lay together. I missed Danielle incredibly, despite realizing that our relationship would never have worked out in the long term. Danielle was resigned to her current life.

There was one task I needed to complete before I evacuated the city. It had been on my mind since I moved from Durham to New Orleans two years earlier. When I moved, I brought all the photo albums with pictures of Allison and me. I could not bring myself to throw them out. Despite sitting on the top shelf of a closet, those photos weighed on me. They reminded me of my anger towards Allison for returning her engagement ring and the betrayal of sleeping with another man so soon after our breakup. Two years later, that anger still raged in my mind.

With a shopping bag in each hand, I walked past the mile-long New Orleans convention center towards the French Quarter. Store owners hammered plywood over their windows. I crossed Canal Street and climbed a short staircase behind Café Du Monde to reach the Mississippi River. Usually, this area would be filled with street performers and art vendors. Today, the area was void of people.

I walked along the bank of the Mississippi, passing through the series of levees that would hopefully protect the city from the hurricane. Two high school students held hands, watching the water flow by. How nice for love to be that easy. There were no thoughts of long-term relationships. They enjoyed being together, day after day.

I passed an older man dressed in a gray suit with a black fedora. He had a weathered face and looked like a native New Orleanian. He chewed tobacco and spat a piece of black tar on the ground. He nodded as I walked by, seemingly unaffected by the news of the storm.

I kept walking, looking for a place where no one would see me. The cement path jogged to the left as I strode along the river. In a crook of the river, a retaining wall hid me from view. This was the place.

I set down my shopping bags and took out a shoebox filled with pictures. These were photos of Allison and me that had accumulated over the four years of our relationship. There were pictures of us holding hands in front of the Roman Colosseum, swimming in the Atlantic Ocean, and standing on the deck of a cruise ship, the Caribbean stretching out behind us. I took a handful of pictures from the box and threw them into the Mississippi. They quickly disappeared out of sight. I took another handful of photos out of the shoebox and saw a picture of Allison and me in Puerto Rico, standing in front of a waterfall. I threw it like a Frisbee into the water. The next picture I saw was us in Times Square on New Year's Eve. Despite below-freezing temperatures, we braved the cold to watch the ball drop. Allison's nose was bright red in the picture. We were both smiling, wearing gaudy plastic glasses, blowing noisemakers, and looking as foolish as all the tourists on New Year's Eve. I tore that photo in half before throwing it into the river. With only a few pictures left, I threw the entire shoebox into the water. It sank briefly, then bobbed to the top and floated towards the Gulf of Mexico.

I knew I was breaking some laws by throwing these photos into the Mississippi River, but I would claim a religious exemption. This was a cleansing, an emotional baptism. I needed Allison out of my life; it was time for a fresh start. With the box gone, I threw a pair of framed eight-by-ten photos into the water.

There were four photo albums in the other shopping bag. I had made the albums for Allison on her birthday to remember our times together. They chronicled our trips, our celebrations, and our milestones. I felt like I couldn't throw the entire album into the Mississippi at once, so I started tearing the pages out and throwing them into the river one by one. This felt like a Band-Aid being slowly pulled off, so after I had ripped out half the pages, I pitched the rest of the album into the river. I threw a few other objects into the Mississippi that Allison had given me during our relationship:

a watch with my initials engraved into the back, a leather wallet, and a book with an inscription.

I dug deep into the bag to find the last item: her engagement ring. Not the whole ring. I had already sold the diamond to recoup some of the money I had spent on it. I could feel the hard ground under my knee as I kneeled to put that ring on Allison's finger. I took the ring and chucked it into the middle of the river. It hit the water without a sound. It was too small to affect the mighty Mississippi.

I pulled out my phone. One picture of Danielle was stored in the photo app. I also needed to make a break from that relationship too. I considered throwing the phone in the river, but that seemed radical. I deleted the photo, then went into the trash to permanently delete it. Danielle was now also out of my life.

As I walked back to my apartment, the high school couple and the older man had disappeared, replaced by an unkempt man strumming an acoustic guitar. His eyes were closed, as if he felt at one with the music.

When I arrived at my apartment, I was ready to leave. A weight had been lifted off me. I had already put my suitcases in my LeBaron and cleaned out my refrigerator in anticipation of the coming blackouts.

On my ride out of New Orleans, I was free of anger and resentment for the first time in a long time. I had rid myself of my relationships with Danielle and Allison. From now on, I would not equate sexual attraction to emotional compatibility. I would find a partner with whom I had both. Maybe not as physically intense as Danielle or as emotionally connected as Allison, but a balance of the two.

I sat quietly as the traffic inched forward out of the city. My baptism in the Mississippi had made me feel reborn. New Orleans was my new home; Durham was a forgotten memory.

ABOUT THE AUTHOR

You can reach the author at adam.lawrence.author@gmail.com
If you enjoyed the book, please leave a review on Amazon or Goodreads.

— · —

COMING SOON

Adam's life continues in **<u>Unwell</u>** coming in Fall 2025